HER CARTEL DADDY

NEW YORK MAFIA DOMS

BIANCA COLE

CONTENTS

I've admired him from afar for years, until he shows his true colors.

Dante Ortega has played guitar at the club I work at ever since I started. His band is famous in New York City. One night, I find out the gorgeous guitarist has a very dark secret.

One moment I'm a bartender living a normal life. The next, I'm kidnapped by the man of my dreams. I'm a witness to a murder he committed. It turns out Dante is the leader of the cartel in New York.

My life is turned upside down faster than I can blink. His touch is as cruel as it is gentle. The chemistry between us is impossible to deny and always has been. Now that the secret is out, he wants to cross the line and make me his.

He won't take no for an answer, and his tastes are anything but vanilla. Will I still want him now I know the darkness that lies within?

VIOLET

The fragrant aroma of fajitas and burritos cooking in the kitchen waft through the bar, making my stomach rumble.

I love the food here. Enrique is an amazing cook. It's the best Mexican food in the city for sure, and we have the best margaritas too.

"Hey, can I get a double scotch on the rocks, doll?" An older man shouts at me, and his breath stinks of alcohol. The happy hour always brings in the worst customers imaginable.

"Coming up," I say, turning around to get him his drink.

The beautiful sound of Dante's guitar fills the bar as he plays solo. The relaxing and soothing sound helps ease my irritation at being spoken to with no respect. It wouldn't hurt him to have some respect for someone who's serving him.

The best night of the week that I work is Friday night, and it's because Dante's band is here.

I pour the double scotch in a glass with ice and pass it to him. "That's four dollars, please."

The guy slaps a five-dollar bill down. "I'll need the change."

Of course he will. Anyone drinking at happy hour always wants their change. I can't wait for it to be over and for the decent customers to arrive. Tips are what I rely on living on minimum wage in New York City. It's not exactly the cheapest place to live in the country.

As I give him is dollar change, he mutters something about slow service. I grit my teeth and hold back my anger. Tonight is going to be a long night.

My eyes move to the beautiful Hispanic guitarist playing on the stage. The rest of the members of his band, The Ortegas, haven't arrived yet. Dante always arrives early to set up.

I can't keep my eyes off the man I've lusted after for two years. He has played at this bar with his band since before I started working here. There is something so sexy about a man with a guitar and tattoos.

His band wasn't well known two years ago, but now they are renowned across the city. I can't help but wonder why after two years of obvious flirting, he's never asked me out. Maybe a bartender isn't good enough for a man like him.

Friday nights are always the highlight of my week because I get to see him. It's a challenge to keep my eyes off him whenever he is here. The way his fingers move effortlessly over the strings with such practiced precision.

His dark brown eyes light up the moment he has his guitar in his hands, seemingly transported into his own world. The dim lights cast him in an ethereal glow and make him look more flawless.

His dark hair is always neat and kept short, and his facial hair is impeccable. The scar across his left eyebrow and the tattoos on his forearms give him a rough, bad boy look. My two biggest weaknesses when it comes to Dante Ortega are his dark chestnut brown eyes and his accent.

I tear my eyes away from the stunning man and focus on stocking the Budweiser up in the fridges beneath the bar before it gets busy. Carlos, my boss, wouldn't be happy if he caught me slacking when there's work to do. He doesn't turn up often, but when he does, it's always unannounced.

He's not the kind of man you want to piss off, as he will fire you on the spot. Carlos has a temper I've witnessed on more than one occasion in the last two years, and I have no intention of being on the wrong end of his wrath.

I open up a few new boxes of beer bottles, stocking up the fridges below the bar. The perfect time to get ahead of the rush, which will be on us before we know it.

Lastly, I check that the kegs connected to the beer taps aren't running low or need changing. Thankfully they don't, as I hate trying to haul them up from the basement on my own.

When I'm finished, I grab my bottle of water and lean against the bar, watching the man of my dreams. He's played the lead in far too many of my fantasies. My friends say I need to ask him out or get over it, as I've not dated anyone since I met him.

No man lives up to Dante. I can't bring myself to ask him out. A man like him wouldn't be interested in a down-and-out bartender like me. What do I have to offer a man like him? His band is up and coming with a huge following, meaning he can get any girl he wants. My fear of rejection is too intense.

He finishes playing his song and I wonder if it's his last one. My stomach flips, and I keep my attention on the bar, knowing that he will be heading over here for a drink if he's finished. Dante is like clockwork.

He comes in alone every Friday and plays solo for half an hour before approaching the bar for a chat and a drink. The highlight of my Friday night.

I glance up at the stage, and our eyes meet as he starts to play another song. My body sets on fire from his gaze. It feels like all the oxygen is sucked out of the air. Every week we dance this same dance together. The heat between us only seems to increase the longer we flirt, but he's never made a move. It's disappointing.

I can only hope that he'll break the ice one day. However, two years of waiting for him to stop flirting and start acting is ebbing away at my hope.

Maybe my friends are right, and I need to move on and get over this crush. I know without a doubt that I do not imagine the chemistry between us, but perhaps it is how he is with women. Musicians are renowned for being players.

Someone nudges me in the side, startling me. "Stop daydreaming about the man you're never going to make a move on and get back to work," Alice says.

I smile at my friend, roommate and colleague. "Hey, I didn't see you come in. Don't worry. I've done all the prep for tonight."

4

She raises a brow. "If only you could see how obvious you are when you are drooling over Dante. It's embarrassing."

"Don't be a dick. I'm not the only one," I say, glancing at the loyal female fans already gathered in front of him.

She laughs. "I'm only messing with you. I wish you'd ask him out, though."

I shake my head. "No chance. He wouldn't be interested."

She grabs a used glass off the counter and shoves it under the bar in the cage for washing. "The way that man looks at you, there's zero chance of him rejecting you."

My cheeks heat, and I clear my throat. "How did your date go with Jared last night?"

She rolls her eyes. "It was Jake, not Jared, and it went better than I expected." She shrugs. "I'm seeing him again tomorrow night."

"You must like him then to agree on a second date." In the two years since I've known Alice, she has been on countless first dates but never a second.

"He is so attractive but also down to earth. It's rare to find a guy like that, so yeah, I do like him."

The asshole I'd served earlier slams his hand down on the bar. "Quit this chit chat and serve me a damn drink."

I grit my teeth. "Same again?"

He nods, grumbling under his breath as I take the glass from him and wash it at the sink before pouring him another double scotch.

I check my watch, noticing it's ten minutes after happy hour, but that this guy wouldn't pay full whack for the drink. "Four dollars."

In quarters and the one dollar bill I'd given him in change earlier, he counts the four dollars out onto the bar. "That's four," he says.

I count it and put it in the cash register, charging him for a single scotch since the cashier prices have changed. Carlos would be pissed if he knew I undercharged the guy after happy hour finished. It's not worth the grief with customers like this guy.

Alice lowers her voice. "Happy hour is over, don't let Carlos catch you doing that."

I shake my head. "I know, but the guy wouldn't pay full price, and it's not worth the argument over ten minutes."

She nods. "True, just don't get caught."

She doesn't need to tell me that. Elena, one of the other bartenders who no longer works here, got caught serving her friends for half price. Carlos withheld her entire week's pay, dismissing her on the spot. He's relentless and unforgiving. The kind of guy you don't want to find yourself on the wrong side of, but this is an entirely different scenario.

Carlos wouldn't admit it to me, but I'm his favorite bartender. He can rely on me without fail to turn up, unlike a lot of my colleagues. It pays the bills, and that's all that matters.

Jenny approaches me. "Hey Violet, did you switch the keg of Budweiser?"

I shake my head. "No, it didn't need changing."

She shakes her head. "It won't last the night. Best to switch it now, so we don't have to do it when we are busy."

I sigh heavily, knowing we have this same argument every

time we're on together. "Carlos would kill us if he knew we pulled a quarter full keg off the bar. You can't do that, I've told you."

Jenny narrows her eyes. "We can't afford to mess about with switching the kegs when it's busy. It will piss off the customers. Carlos would agree." She shakes her head. "We can put the barrel back on for tomorrow's happy hour."

"Do what you want, Jenny." I know that arguing with her never gets me anywhere. It's best to let her do it and blame her if Carlos gets angry.

She huffs as if she expected me to go down and change the kegs before walking away. I do most of the preparation work every night I'm in. The woman is lazy and needs to learn the meaning of hard work.

I sigh heavily and rest against the back bar, returning my attention to Dante as he strums his guitar. For a moment, all my worries melt away as I listen to the calming sound of his voice filling the room. He makes working here and dealing with this shit worth it.

2

DANTE

The only escape from the darkness of my life is Friday night playing this bar with my band. Even as our popularity increases, we still play here every Friday night without fail. Ric wanted to ditch it, but I call the shots. There's one reason I didn't want to stop playing here, and that reason has her eyes on me like she always does.

I take a break from playing solo, propping my guitar up against the wall of the bar. The stunning bartender, Violet, who I can't cross the line with. Carlos, the bar owner and one of my distributors for the cartel, wouldn't be best pleased if I fucked his employee.

He wouldn't dare question me, but I know not to cross that line. Not to mention she may lust after me, but she doesn't want to be pulled into my world.

Music is my escape. The other side of my life is dark and twisted. A life that isn't built for a woman like Violet.

As the leader of the cartel, I live by a set of rules that I never break. Never bring anyone not already in the game into it. Sleeping with someone like her is violating that rule.

I can't deny that I've been tempted on more than one occasion to take her home with me, but if there's one thing I'm good at, it's sticking to the rules. You don't run the cartel operations in New York for as long as I have without being disciplined.

Violet looks up at me, and our eyes connect. I feel my cock getting hard instantly as that electricity pulses through the air between us. It's a miracle that I've managed to stop myself from pushing her up against the wall and fucking her senseless in the back of this bar.

We've met in the tight confines of the back room and hall-ways of El Torero multiple times. It's taken every fiber of my willpower to resist taking her in public—one of my favorite kinks.

I walk toward her, shoving my hands in my pockets to hide the desire attempting to surface. It's time for a drink. Francisco, Ric, and Javier will be here in ten minutes. I intend to spend the rest of the time I've got alone, chatting to the object of my desires.

"Buenos dias, señorita," I say in greeting, smiling as her cheeks flush when I speak to her.

"Hey, Dante," she says, wiping down the bar. "Can I get you something to drink?"

She knows I always drink rum, but she always asks me. "A large rum on the rocks."

Violet raises a brow. "Don't want to change it up and have something different for once?"

I sit on the stool in front of her. "Why change something that works?"

She shrugs. "Makes life more exciting if you aren't predictable all the time."

I run a hand across my jaw. "Are you calling me predictable, Miss. Kenzie?" I've been called many things in my life, but predictable isn't one of them.

She shrugs. "I don't know a lot about you, but when it comes to Friday night, you seem to stick to a routine."

I smile. "You pay a lot of attention to my routine, do you, señorita?

Her cheeks flush a deep red, and she looks away from me, shaking her head. "I just mean you get here at the same time and always order the same drink." She meets my gaze. "You play the same solo songs on your guitar, too."

I swallow hard, knowing that she pays as much attention to me as I pay to her. "I'll bear that in mind for future reference. Maybe I'll play something different for you next week." I wink at her, and she looks away, shaking her head.

"Don't listen to me." She sets a large rum in front of me with ice. "If there's something that works for you, then you should stick with it."

Little does my princess know that my entire life is unpredictable. The only stability is my Friday nights at this bar, where I enjoy the predictability of the evening.

"I may shake things up a little bit on your recommendation, bonita." I flash her a smile, and the blush on her cheeks spreads down her neck. I love seeing the way I'm under her skin so deeply.

Although, it makes keeping away from her more difficult. She's pure temptation, and I'm a sinner, not a saint. Keeping my distance from her is growing more difficult.

"Are you looking forward to tonight's gig?" She asks, trying to change the subject.

I lean back in the barstool, bringing the rum to my lips and sipping on it. "Very much. I love playing our gig here." Part of me wants to tell her I love playing for her, as she's the main motivation for keeping our spot at this bar. I know that is too dangerous to admit. It's only a matter of time until she makes a move if I keep up my flirting.

I'm surprised she hasn't already. I know we should never get involved, but I hold onto hope she might make the move. The thought of her lips on mine drives me wild, but it will have to remain a fantasy.

"Why do you always arrive before the rest of the band?" Violet asks, tilting her head to the side.

I shrug. "I like to warm up my hands and vocal cords. The rest of the band aren't as dedicated as me." The only thing I'm dedicated to on a Friday night is spending the spare moments I have talking to Violet. "I notice you rarely have a Friday night off. Doesn't a girl like you have a lot of plans on Friday nights?"

She shakes her head, cheeks growing red. "No. I've got to work and pay the bills." She grabs a cloth and starts to wipe down the bar for the second time since I sat down.

I can't help but smile as I'm not stupid. This bar is open

seven nights a week, and she could take off a Friday and work a Sunday night instead. In the two years since she started working here, she's taken two Friday nights off.

"Don't lie, I know it's because you love listening to us." My comment only turns her cheeks a deeper red. It's obvious that she works every Friday to see me. Violet has been my biggest temptation for the last two years—a temptation that gets more and more difficult to resist each week that passes by.

She's beyond beautiful. Maybe I'll cave one night and kiss her perfect, plump lips that I've longed to claim ever since I set eyes on her.

"Is Carlos coming in tonight?" I ask. Carlos owes me a shitload of money and has been avoiding me. He may be a friend and distributor for the cartel, but friendship only goes so far.

She shrugs. "The boss never tells me when he's coming in. I think he likes to keep us on our toes."

I laugh. "Probably. The guy can be an asshole."

Her eyes widen, but she doesn't argue. I get the feeling Carlos isn't liked among his staff. He's not liked among his friends, let alone people that have to work for him.

"Como te va, amigo?" Ricardo says behind me, clapping me on the shoulder.

I glance at my friend, wishing that my time alone with Violet wasn't over. It felt way too quick tonight, but as always, our short moments alone always end too quickly.

"Soy bueno y tu?"

He nods in response. "I'm good. Am I the first one here?"

I knock back the rest of my rum. "Yes, Javier and Francisco haven't arrived yet."

Ric sighs. "They're always late, those assholes." He glances at Violet. "Can you get me a beer, señorita?"

I hate the way he talks to Violet as if she's below him, like a piece of meat. He treats all women like that, but I don't care when it's any other woman.

"Coming right up, Ric," she says, grabbing him a beer.

I find myself watching her every move—every little quirk of hers as she nervously flicks her golden blonde hair over her shoulder. The way she always nervously tugs at the edge of her shirt when she is speaking to me. Everything about her is attractive.

I need remember Violet isn't part of my world, and that makes her untouchable. The danger of anyone learning the truth about me means that even Violet isn't worth the risk. Javier is next to enter the bar, and he comes straight for me.

"Jefe, I've been trying to get a hold of you for an hour."

My brow furrows as I dig out my phone. "Shit, sorry. I had it on silent as I was performing. Anything urgent?"

Javier sighs. "We'll discuss it after the show."

I nod and knock back the rest of my rum. "It's almost time to go on. Where is Francisco?"

"No idea. Hey, Violet. Can I get a beer?"

She smiles at him with the most beautiful smile. "Of course."

I can't take my eyes off her as she goes to fetch him his drink. "¡Ella está buena," I mutter, loud enough for Javier to hear.

He claps me on the back. "When are you going to fuck that girl out of your system and move on?"

I glare at my friend and lugarteniente. "You know I wouldn't cross that line."

Javier rolls his eyes. "Fuck knows why not." He never agreed with my keeping it in the game rule, and I understand why. That leaves me with only whores to fuck, but that's better than getting involved with someone real.

"Hola, Amigos," Francisco says, coming in late.

I spin around on my bar stool. "What time do you call this?"

He looks at his watch. "Looks like right on time if you ask me."

I shake my head. "Why can't you ever get here a few minutes before?" Francisco is the least reliable of my closest men by far, but he's also the most brutal. I can trust him to get shit done for me that most men couldn't even dream of.

He laughs. "Punctuality is my forte. I don't need to be here early, just exactly on time."

I roll my eyes and set down the glass on the bar. "Time to rock and roll." I meet Violet's gaze, which is hot and heavy with desire—desire that drives me wild.

I give her a wink, which turns her cheeks a deep pink again. It takes all my willpower to tear my gaze away from her and head toward the stage.

3

VIOLET

The night is drawing to a close as The Ortegas play their last song. The place is packed and always is when they're here.

I take a pause and lean against the bar, thankful that it's past midnight, meaning no more customers to serve. The bar is licensed to serve alcohol up to midnight. My attention moves to Dante, who, in my eyes, is the star of the band. He's not lead vocals, that's Ric, but this song he is singing in his beautiful voice that raises goosebumps over every inch of my skin.

Dante is perfection. He's gorgeous and beyond talented. I know I'm not the only woman in this city that has the hots for the guitarist. The band has a loyal female following, but Dante is the only heartthrob, in my opinion.

Everyone erupts into applause as Dante finishes the song, his eyes coming up and meeting mine across the crowd. I shudder, looking down at the bar quickly as he's caught me staring at him on more than one occasion tonight.

"Hey, can I get another beer?" Some guy shouts at me, forcing me to look up.

I glance at my watch. "We called last orders twenty minutes ago." I shake my head. "I'm sorry, I can't serve you."

His eyes narrow, and he slams his hands down on the counter. "Oh, fuck off. It's a beer."

I grit my teeth, noticing the guy is already pretty drunk. "We're not licensed to serve alcohol after midnight. I'm sorry."

He stands from the stool, towering over me. "I said one beer, now serve me it, bitch."

Dante isn't as tall as the guy being an asshole, but he appears to one side, eyes full of rage as he overheard him. He sets a hand on the guy's shoulder. "Leave her alone."

My heart skips a beat hearing him come to my rescue. The asshole that called me a bitch shakes his head. "Or what?" He turns to face Dante, and I notice his shoulders tense as he bows his head. "I'm sorry, Dante. I didn't realize it was you."

Dante's eyes narrow as he glances between the guy and me. "I don't think it's me you need to be apologizing to, Hernandez. Apologize to Violet now."

My cheeks heat over Dante's heroic rescue. I don't need his apology. "It doesn't matter. I'm used to it," I say, grabbing an empty glass off the bar counter and sliding it into a crate under the bar for the washer. That's been the truth for a long time before I moved to New York and became a bartender. My stepdad was an abusive drunk, the kind of guy you'd find in this bar at happy hour.

Dante shakes his head. "I don't care what you are used to. He disrespected you in front of me." He grabs the guy's shoulder. "Apologize."

Hernandez turns to face me, throat bobbing as he swallows hard. "I'm sorry for speaking to you as I did."

There is a tension in the air that is impossible to put into words. Dante Ortega oozes power, even if he is just a guitarist in a band. There's something different about him that I can't put my finger on.

I nod at the guy in response, feeling awkward that he's been forced to apologize. If it weren't for Dante, he would probably still be pushing me to serve him after our licensed hours.

"Now fuck off," Dante says.

I'm surprised when he listens to him and turns around, leaving us alone. Dante's dark brown eyes are intense as they lock onto mine. "If anyone gives you any trouble, Violet. You tell me, alright?"

I nod but feel a little uncomfortable with the way he got that guy to apologize. It was a daunting side to him I've never seen before, even if the guy was a jerk.

He bangs his palms down on the bar. "Is the bar shut for us?" he asks, nodding his head toward Ric, who is approaching.

Carlos always instructs me to give the band drinks even after the last orders. I shake my head. "No, what do you want?"

"Rum on the rocks for me." Dante glances at Ric. "What are you having?"

"I'll have a beer."

I nod. "Coming right up." I turn to fetch their drinks. Ric is the joker of the band, but he's a nice guy. All of the band members are nice guys, unlike some of the other artists that play here. They're by far the most well know but the least egotistical.

I set the beer down in front of Ric and the rum in front of Dante. "You guys were amazing as always," I say, trying to avoid making eye contact with Dante. "I think Enrique left some food in the kitchen for you."

I can feel his attention burning a hole in me as I wipe down the bar as a way to distract myself from him. It's ridiculous how hot his presence makes me.

"Can't beat Enrique's enchiladas," Ric says, leaning over the bar a bit. "On another note, which one of us was the best tonight, though, Violet?"

I shake my head, meeting Ric's gaze. "You were all equally amazing."

Dante smirks. "You can't back out of answering. Who is your favorite?"

My cheeks heat. "I've got no favorites. I love the band, not the individuals."

Dante raises a brow as if he knows how much I love him. I wish I hadn't said the word love, as it feels awkward as hell. He watches me with such intensity—an intensity that makes my stomach flutter.

"Are you sure I'm not your favorite, Vi?" Dante says, calling me by a nickname only he uses.

I shake my head. "Nope," I say, turning away and busying

myself with cleaning the bar. My cheeks are burning with embarrassment, which means they will be bright red.

There's a tension in the air you could cut with a knife. I turn back around once the embarrassment wears off, knocking into Jenny. "Watch where you are going," she says.

Dante growls softly. "You were the one not watching where you were going," he says.

Her eyes widen, and she swallows hard before walking on.

I shake my head. "Thanks for the assist, but Jenny is always a jerk."

Dante nods. "I hate people like that. Are you sure you don't know when Carlos will be in next?" Dante asks.

My brow furrows as he's been pushing about when Carlos will be in all night. "No, he doesn't tell me." I turn around and face him. "Have you tried ringing him?"

He gives me an odd look, tilting his head slightly. "I'm not sure I've got his most recent number. Have you got it?"

I shrug. "It might be in the office. I'll take a look."

Dante holds a hand up. "Don't worry. I'll take a look on my way to the kitchen." He glances at Ric. "We best pack up."

I shake my head. "Carlos doesn't allow people, other than staff, into the office."

Dante smirks. "Do you think that applies to me as his friend?"

"I have no idea." I shrug. "I'll go in and check for his number in the office." I catch Alice's attention. "Are you alright cleaning up for a moment while I head into the office?"

She nods. "Of course, you did all the prep tonight. I can

handle the tidying up." Her eyes move to Dante, and when he's not looking, she winks.

My cheeks heat as he can't go in the office but I kind of wish he would. Time alone with him always gets my fantasies running wild. "I'll be back in a moment," I say to Dante.

He shakes his head and pulls up the hatch in the bar, walking the other side. "I'm coming with you, señorita. I've got some enchiladas to pick up."

I lead the way into the back of the club. Carlos wouldn't be happy that I let him back here, friend or not. Normally, I'm supposed to bring the food out to the band.

Dante follows me closely as we walk into the back of the bar, making the hair on the back of my neck stand on end.

We pass the kitchen, which still smells amazing. Enrique leaves the bartenders something tasty for dinner. He's so thoughtful, even though Carlos wouldn't approve.

I stop at the office door and open it, glancing back at Dante, who is closer than I anticipated. His dark eyes are fixed on me with an intensity that makes my stomach twist.

I clear my throat and step inside, walking for the desk as that's where Carlos keeps important numbers. His number is on a post-it on the computer, and I grab it, turning around to find Dante inches from me. He towers over me, and the heady, musky scent of him overtakes my senses.

My legs wobble beneath me, and I feel unsteady. "Here's the number," I say, awkwardly shoving it into Dante's hard chest.

He doesn't take the number. Instead, he stares at me with fire blazing in his eyes. "Vi," he says my name, moving slightly closer to me so that our bodies are pressed together. "You look stunning tonight."

My brow furrows. "I'm wearing the same outfit I wear every time you see me."

His jaw clenches, and he lowers his head closer to mine. "I don't mean your outfit. You always look stunning."

I can hardly breathe right now, wondering if he's going to make a move. The air is thick with sexual tension.

"Tell me what you want, bonita."

I swallow, knowing that I couldn't trust myself to speak right now. My stomach is fluttering, and all I can do is stare at the man of my dreams dumbfounded.

Dante slips a hand onto my hip and leans toward me, brushing his lips against my cheek softly. "I want to kiss you, Vi."

My heart rate accelerates. Is this finally about to happen? To think I almost insisted he didn't come with me.

"Dante," I murmur his name.

He teases his hand up to my throat and squeezes softly. "Call me daddy, princess," he growls into my ear.

A shot of electric excitement consumes me, and I gasp a little, shocked by him asking me to call him that. My nipples harden painfully, and my pussy gets wet instantly. "Yes, daddy," I breathe. It's so dirty but feels so right, and I love the way he orders me about.

He groans and moves his lips to mine, kissing me passionately. Our lips meld together in a kiss that holds such pent-up desire.

His tongue teases against my lips, seeking entrance.

BIANCA COLE

We shouldn't be doing this at all, let alone in Carlos's office. I'm too weak to stop. My lips part, allowing his tongue inside my mouth as he deepens the kiss. My panties are soaking wet as I feel his hot, hard body against mine.

Dante grabs my hips possessively and lifts me onto the edge of the desk, stepping between my thighs. I feel the hard press of his cock through his pants as he moves a hand to my throat and squeezes. I moan like a wanton whore, wanting nothing more than to feel every inch of him buried as deep as possible inside of me.

I submit to the sensation, loving the way his dominance makes me feel. Dante wants me the way I want him, and I've never wanted a man so badly.

He kisses my neck, increasing the heat building inside of me. I run my hand through his short dark hair, moaning.

Footsteps approaching the office followed by Ric's voice startles the both of us apart. "Where the fuck is my enchilada?"

I'm breathing heavily and so hot I'm sure my face is bright red. If Ric were to walk in here right now, he'd know what we'd been up to.

Dante swallows, and a look of guilt passes through his eyes as he meets my gaze. "We best get back." He grabs the post-it note off the desk with Carlos's number on it. "Thanks for the number." He waves it and then walks away from me, leaving me gawping after him like an idiot.

I can't believe he finally kissed me. A kiss that most certainly didn't disappoint. The pent-up longing between us is so intense that our brief moment of passion was hotter than anything I could have imagined.

I shouldn't be so happy about one lousy kiss, but I can't help it. Dante has haunted my dreams for too long, and maybe those dreams are finally coming true. The only thing I'm disappointed about is that it didn't go any further.

4

DANTE

I pack away my guitar in its case and carry it out the back of the club to the band's van. Ric is putting the drums away, and he glances up as I come out. "Good night, Dante?" He asks.

I shrug and walk past him. Ric is a bit of a clown, and I don't like to indulge him when he has had a drink. All of the band work for me and my operation here in New York. My father is the head of the cartel, and he runs the operation in Mexico, leaving me to head up the stateside business. It runs smoothly, and no one would dare question the Ortega family's supremacy.

Tonight was a good night until I fucked up and kissed Violet. I've managed to keep control of my urges, but when I had her there alone in that office, the temptation was too great. It was a mistake that I can't let happen again.

"Are you sure we still want to keep this gig?" Ric asks, approaching me as I slide the guitar case into the back of the van. "Isn't it below us to be playing this bar now that we're so sought after?"

I grit my teeth. "Riccardo, we've had this exact conversation more than once. Are you trying to anger me?"

He holds his hands up. "I'm just saying that I can't see the reason we are keeping the gig." He tilts his head slightly. "Other than the hot piece of ass you still haven't asked out working behind the bar."

I snap, grabbing the collar of his shirt. "Think carefully, Ric, if you are talking about Violet," I growl.

He pales but holds my gaze. "Tell me I'm wrong then."

He's not wrong, but I'm too proud to admit that the reason I keep this gig is because of her. Not only would it be dangerous for her, but it would also appear weak, something I never allow.

"Don't argue with me about it. You know Carlos is a friend, and I like playing here." I search his eyes. "Got it?"

Ric nods. "Yeah, understood. Now fucking let me go."

I let go of his collar and pace away from him. Ric and Javier are the only guys I'd allow to question me like that. We all grew up together. My father and Ric's father were friends before the enemy killed him in a drive-by, and we have a mutual respect that my position in the cartel can't break.

"I had a call from the Mercury Lounge. It could be great for the band, and they want us to play next Friday."

I grit my teeth. Ric isn't going to let this go easily, but the decision to merge our love for music and laundering money was simply that. We can launder money as band earnings amongst the many other businesses we run through the city.

"We draw enough attention as it is. Remember why we set the band up in the first place and drop it. We are not changing gigs."

Ric sighs heavily, and I know this is far from over. As we quarrel about the gig at the Mercury Lounge, I don't notice Miguel, a low-level drug dealer, who thinks he's more important than he is, approaching.

"Dante and Riccardo. How are you, my friends?" He asks.

I turn to face him, clenching my fists by my side to stop myself from reaching for the gun. Miguel has some balls to come and approach me at all, let alone call me a friend. "What the fuck do you want, Miguel?"

Miguel's brow furrows as if he was expecting a big welcome. "More territory. I'm by far the best dealer you have on your books, and I deserve recognition for my achievements."

I glance at Ric, who is smirking. He knows what happened to the last drug dealer who thought he deserved more from me. He was dead before he could blink.

"Is that so?" I ask.

Miguel nods. "Yeah, if you check the sales records, I'm outperforming any of the other salesmen."

I scoff at that. "Salesmen?" I glance at Ric. "Can you believe this guy?"

He shakes his head slowly. "No, I think he needs to be taught what his place is in this organization."

Miguel's eyes widen, and he pales, realizing only now the big mistake he made approaching me with this bullshit.

I nod in response. "Yes, he needs to be taught." I draw the gun from my holster and cock the gun, pointing it at his head.

Miguel takes a step backward, holding his hands up. "I didn't want any trouble."

I feel the darkness infecting my blood. Friday night is the one night that I escape from this part of my life, but this asshole made sure I couldn't escape this week.

"Well, trouble is what you found," Ric says, stepping closer to the idiot. "Why on earth would you think you could come and demand anything from Dante Ortega?" I ask.

Miguel stutters, not making any sense. He's shaking like a leaf. "Don't do this, Dante. I didn't mean to disrespect you."

I exchange one last glance with my friend before pulling the trigger and shooting him right through the head. The shot kills him in one as he collapses on the floor.

The gasp behind me makes my heart still in my chest. I turn around to see Violet standing at the club's back door, holding a tied-up bag of trash. Her eyes are wide as she stands there, frozen in shock, staring at Miguel's body.

Fuck.

The woman I've lusted after for two years is now a witness to a murder I committed. It leaves me with no other choice but to kidnap her.

Ric meets my gaze and nods as though he can read my mind. Hell, he probably can. I've known the guy since I was five years old.

"Violet, I can explain," I say, stepping toward her with my hands out in surrender.

She shakes her head, slowly backing away from me. "Don't come any closer," she says, her voice shaky.

I'm dealing with a deer ready to bolt at any moment. Every action I take has to be well thought out as a scared witness reaching anyone else is dangerous. Violet has switched from a guilty desire to a threat so fast that I can hardly process it.

"Violet, please let me explain."

She shakes her head again before turning and running back toward the bar.

"Fuck," I growl, rushing in after her. She can't outrun me, especially not in her heels.

Violet barely makes it inside by the time I've wrapped my arms around her waist, lifting her effortlessly.

She thrashes in my arms, shouting as I struggle to force my hand over her mouth. Once I've got my hand over her mouth, she stills.

"Stop this, now," I say, keeping my voice calm, despite the chaos rising inside of me. I carry Violet back out toward the van, knowing that I only have one option. Ric is already getting the restraints out of the back of the van.

I hate the fear I see in her eyes. It replaces all of that hot, passionate desire she regarded me with only half an hour ago when I saved her from the asshole at the bar and then kissed her.

Ric approaches, not needing me to tell him what to do. He

slides the gag over her head, forcing it into her mouth and tying it tight. Then he grabs her arms forcefully, tying the rope tight around her wrists tighter than I would. I notice her wince.

The twisting sensation in my gut makes me clench my jaw as I watch Ric handle her roughly. There's a possessiveness inside of me that is born out of my infatuation for Violet.

It looks like Ric is about to get everything he wanted, as now Violet is my captive. There's no need to play this bar anymore.

Violet's eyes are fill of panic as he sits her down in the back of our van. Francisco and Javier, my two other band members, approach. They hardly bat an eye at the dead body on the floor, and the woman bound and gagged in the back of our band's van.

"Looks like some bad shit went down," Javier says.

Francisco nods. "Need a hand getting the body in the back of the van?"

I clench my jaw, meeting Violet's gaze. The fear in them cuts me, and the thought of placing a dead, bloody body in the back of the van with her makes my stomach churn. My princess is about to learn how dark my life is.

Now that she is part of the game, there's no going back. A witness can't be allowed to be free. She's my captive.

"Yes, get out a body bag and put him in the back." I glance at Javier. "Get a guy down to clear up. We will have to go via the factory before heading home."

Javier nods, his face grave as he pulls out his cell phone to make the call. None of us like visiting the factory to dispose of bodies. It's a gruesome task, but the only way to properly dispose of a body is in vats of acid to ensure nothing can be traced back to us.

Miguel is an asshole. He brought this on himself, approaching me and trying to demand more fucking money.

Who does he think he is?

No one is stupid enough to demand anything from me, at least not anyone who is still breathing today.

Francisco places the body bag by the side of Miguel's body and shifts him into it with Ric's help. They zip the bag up and then lift it into the back of the van, sliding it in next to Violet. I watch her eyes widen as she tries to shift away from the bag.

The tears spilling down her cheeks grate at me more than I can explain. I saved her from an asshole treating her badly at the bar less than an hour ago, and now I have no choice but to kidnap her and treat her far worse. She's escaped the asshole only to fall into the hands of a monster.

I grab the sliding door of the van and slam it shut without another glance at her. It's time to get over my infatuation with the bartender, as there's no chance for a romance now she knows the beast living inside of me.

Ironically, this is my best chance of getting what I want from her, even if she won't be all that willing after learning who I am.

Some women love the life of danger, but Violet doesn't strike me as that type of woman. She's sensible and innocent, everything that I'm not. Now I'll have to twist her into something dark or kill her—the latter isn't an option.

She has been mine since the moment I set eyes on her, and now she's part of my world. There's no escaping the fact. Violet is in the game, and she's never getting out.

5

VIOLET

This situation can't be happening to me.

My world is spinning as I sit in the back of the moving van right next to a body bag housing a man that I saw Dante shoot dead in cold blood. The numbness spreading through my body is unlike anything I've ever felt.

He shot the guy without a moment's hesitation as if it's the kind of thing that he does every day. The cold hard look he gave me as I was forced into the van was the opposite of the fiery, hot desire normally burning in the depths of his dark brown eyes.

I'm numb with shock.

What the hell have I stumbled on?

Dante has kidnapped me. I jolt against the side of the van, and the body bag slides against me. It makes my skin crawl.

For four years, I've been free from the darkness of a life dictated by a bad man. Four years I've been free from anything dark or depraved, and it feels like I'm being dragged back underwater by these assholes. The captivity makes my skin crawl and brings back a flood of unwanted memories I tried to bury a long time ago.

How can they get away with murdering a guy in the street?

The van slows down and turns again. I hear a rough material crunching beneath the tires as the van jerks around another bend before slowing to a stop. I hold my breath as the van's engine cuts off, and the sound of a door opening makes me sick to my stomach.

My heart races frantically as I wait, bound and gagged. At the tender age of twenty-four years old, I get the feeling my life might be quickly nearing its end. I've watched enough crime films to know witnesses don't survive long. The only way to silence a witness is to make sure they are dead and buried.

The door opens to the back of the van, and Dante stands there with a hard expression. He avoids my gaze, glancing at Ric, who stands to his right. "Let's get this over with."

I hold my breath, wondering what they're going to do to me. Ric drags the body bag out of the van with the help of Javier. All the while, Dante watches me with that same cold, hard look that sends shivers down my spine. There's a darkness in him—darkness I'm only now noticing.

They carry the body away, and for a few moments, Dante stares at me. He doesn't say a word as he turns to follow the men with the body, leaving me waiting.

They speak in fast Spanish, which I don't understand. They're getting rid of the body. I'm not sure how. I glance around the back of the van, noticing more body bags stacked at the back.

I squirm a little, managing to move toward the open van door to try and see where we are. My heart skips a beat as I see Dante with his back turned to me standing over a huge vat.

Ric, Javier, and Francisco struggle to lift the body into the vat. I swallow hard, wondering if I'm having one fucked up and realistic nightmare. They're eradicating all evidence of the murder Dante committed out the back of the bar. Anyone could have witnessed it, and I'm shocked that the man I've had a crush on for two years is a killer.

The way they've driven to this abandoned industrial unit and are disposing of the man so calmly suggests this isn't the first time they've killed someone. None of the band batted an eyelid at the dead man or the fact I was tied up in the back of the van.

"Fucking waste of space deserves everything he got," Ric says, placing a lid on the vat and doing it up. "He had the fucking audacity to approach us as if we were his friends."

Dante clears his throat. "Always respectful of the dead, Ric?"

Javier shakes his head. "You can't say a thing, Dante. You killed the guy and have a fucking witness to the murder."

Francisco joins in. "Yeah, what are you going to do with Violet?"

I quickly move backward as he moves to look back at the van. "Let me worry about that."

Ric sighs. "You may be soft on the girl, but you can't keep her alive."

There's a deep, guttural growl, followed by the cocking of a gun. "Are you trying to tell me what I can or can't do, Ric?"

There are a few moments of silence. "Cool it, Dante. You know what the protocol is, and that's all I'm saying."

"Fuck off. I make the damn protocol." I can almost feel the tension from the back of the van. "We may be friends but don't forget your place, Ric."

What kind of shit have I stumbled on?

I hear footsteps approaching and wiggle back into the same position I was in before. My eyes remain fixed to the ground, and I try to stop myself from shaking in fear.

Dante is a murderer, but I get the feeling that is just the tip of the iceberg. "Look at me, girl," Ric says.

I raise my head and meet the gaze of the lead singer. He wants me dead.

"Dante doesn't want me to kill you, so you are lucky he has a soft spot for you." He climbs into the back of the van, making my heart rate accelerate.

I can hardly breathe as he gets nearer—a man that wants to murder me. I've never felt such paralyzing fear in my life. All I can do is stare at the floor, scared to make the smallest movement.

"Ricardo, get the fuck away from her," Dante growls, the anger in his voice is fear inspiring.

"No sé a qué estás jugando, jefe," Ric speaks in Spanish, making it impossible for me to understand.

Dante approaches with a look that could kill. I've never feared anyone the way I fear him. "Cuidado," he says one single word slowly, eyeing Ric with such a threatening gaze.

Ric backs off and walks out of the van, jumping down and saying something in Spanish to the others. Dante moves his gaze to me, and the fire in his eyes makes my stomach churn— a fire that used to set me ablaze. I can't get the image of him pulling that trigger out of my mind.

"Keep quiet, Violet. I'll explain everything to you soon," he says, his voice deep and husky. A sound that used to drive me wild, but now it makes me feel sick.

How can he explain anything I've seen tonight? There is no explanation for what he did. He's a murderer, and there is nothing else to be said.

I gaze at the floor of the van, focusing on a dark red stain, which is more than likely blood. His gaze remains on me, but I can't bring myself to look at him again.

Dante walks away and slams shut the door, making me jump. I feel pain clutch at my chest as tears well in my eyes. If Dante doesn't intend to kill me, what does he intend to do to me?

The tears don't fall. It's as though the shock prevents me from crying. All I can do is stare at the same bloodstain, struggling to bring myself to look away.

Am I broken?

I sure as hell feel like I am. I can hardly process the insane thoughts racing through my mind. All I want to do is ring the police and tell them what I saw. Dante should be locked up in federal prison for what he did. Ric watched as if it was normal too, and then the other two turned up as if this was a standard Friday night.

The Ortegas are a bunch of murderous criminals, and

something tells me I don't know the half of it. It's as though I've woken up in a nightmare. The man I've had a crush on for two years isn't my hero, he's the villain of my story. I shake my head, trying to force the fact to sink in.

He's kidnapped me—taken me against my will.

I can't imagine what his intentions are for me, but I know they can't be good. Unease twists at my gut as I realize just how much darkness I've fought so hard to contain might resurface in this situation. I'm a fighter and always have been, but there are some demons even I'm not brave enough to face again.

All I can do is sit and stare at the bloodstain on the floor, feeling utterly numb as the van drives me to my hellish fate.

6

DANTE

I focus on the road as we drive toward my home on the other side of Queens. Inside I'm a mess. Violet will never understand why I shot that man. She could never understand the world that I operate in. A dark one that an innocent, sweet woman like her doesn't belong to.

My stomach churns as a sick and twisted part of me is glad she saw—glad that she's now my captive. I still want her, perhaps more than ever after the kiss that we shared in Carlos's office. A kiss that was filled with more passion and heat than I could have imagined. I guess that's what happens when you both resist the temptation for so long.

There's no way I'm going to be able to keep my hands off of her when I get her home. Maybe I should send her down to Mexico to my father to deal with. I can't trust myself to handle this properly.

As that thought crosses my mind, a dark rage builds inside of me. I know what my father would do to her, and the thought makes me want to kill him. I clench my fists and try to breathe deeply. If I'm going to handle this properly, I need to get my emotions under control.

Violet doesn't strike me as the kind of señorita that would accept my life willingly. I don't know what I want from her. All I know is that from the moment we met two years ago at Carlos's bar, I haven't been able to think of any other woman. I've fucked women, but even then, it's lost its appeal. I always find myself thinking about Violet.

Ric pulls the van up to the gates of my mansion, which open to allow us in. This is it. We're at my home, and I've got to decide how I'm going to play this. To Violet, I'm a murderous monster, and it's going to take time to restore that adoration she once held for me.

I could take her by force, but that doesn't appeal to me. I want her to want me and kiss me the way she did in that office —as if her life depended on it. Only this time, her life does depend on the way she reacts to the real me—the man darkened by so much pain, suffering, and murder she could hardly begin to imagine.

Ric turns the engine off, and I get out, cracking my neck in an attempt to release the pent of frustration. "I'm going to deal with Violet. You brief the men and check that the men cleared everything up outside the bar."

Ric nods. "Sure thing, boss. Enjoy." He winks.

Ric is an asshole when it comes to women. If he were in

my position, he'd fuck Violet all night long, even if she didn't want it. Even if she screamed and begged for him to stop. He's a sick son of a bitch, but I need men like him by my side. He's one of my lugarteniente for that reason. He's not afraid to get his hands dirty all to protect our family. The Ortega Cartel is a family.

Ric heads toward the mansion, leaving me alone with the van. Violet has been silent in the back the entire time. I take a deep inhale before hardening my gaze and opening the back doors.

Violet is still staring at the bloodstain on the floor of the van. She doesn't look up when I open the door. Maybe I've broken her.

"Out," I bark.

When she doesn't react or stand, I get into the back of the van and grab her wrists hard. Violet needs to learn to obey. Otherwise, there will be dire consequences. I can't let anyone think I'm going soft.

She gasps as I lift her by the ropes around her wrist and drag her out of the van. She squeals behind the gag and tries to fight me.

I grab her throat hard. "You have no power here, Violet. Shut up and do as you're told."

The little color she did have in her cheeks drains away, and she stares at the floor, going limp. Part of me hates treating her like this, and the other part of me loves it—loves forcing her to submit to me.

I grit my teeth and drag her limp body toward the house,

heading straight through the entrance and up the stairs. Ric is in the entrance hall, smirking as he sees me roughly handling the innocent bartender.

Violet doesn't struggle or breathe another word as I lead her to the room adjoining mine. She has no idea the shit show she just landed in. If she did, she wouldn't resist me. It pains me to think I'm going to have to reveal my true colors to the only woman that looks at me so adoringly.

Up until now, she's seen me as a guitarist in a band—plain and simple. Now I'm a murderer in her eyes, and she doesn't know the half of it. It's by far not the first life I've taken and most certainly not the last. Typical that she'd witness something like that after I'd had my first tempting taste of her.

If Ric had his way, Violet would be inside a vat of acid right now, never to be found again. The thought makes me sick to my stomach. She doesn't deserve the treatment she's going to receive, but I have no choice. Her life will change irrevocably from tonight.

Father wouldn't be pleased if he learned that I'd broken protocol, but Ric wouldn't dare go behind my back and tell him—none of my men would. My father trusts me to follow the rules and keeping Violet alive breaks the most vital one of all. Never leave any witnesses alive.

I open the door to my room and shove her inside, turning to shut the door. For a moment, I stare at the door with my back turned, dreading removing her gag. If she asks questions I won't answer with any truth, not unless I want to plunge her into more danger.

When I turn around, Violet has backed to the other side of the room and is staring at me with pure terror. Her desire has turned to hate and fear over something she could never understand.

"Sit down, señorita," I say, nodding toward the bed—a bed I've longed to see her on but in totally different circumstances.

She doesn't move, staring at me with almost disbelief.

I grit my teeth, wishing she'd do as I say. "I said, sit. I won't ask again."

She narrows her eyes slightly before moving carefully toward the bed and sitting.

I walk toward Violet and stand in front of her. She keeps her eyes forward, not meeting my gaze.

"I'm going to remove your gag, and then I'm going to talk, and you are going to listen. Understand?"

She looks up at me and searches my eyes before nodding slowly.

My fingers tingle as I reach for the gag around the back of her neck. I undo the knot and move the fabric out of her mouth.

She gasps for air the moment she's free from the gag, but she doesn't say a word. Her breathing is frantic and heavy. A sound that makes me want to tie her to my bed and make her scream. I know she's scared, but eventually, she will come around to her new existence—an existence of captivity as my property. Violet has no other choice. It's either that or death.

"You will stay here from now on, Violet. I can't let you go back out into the world telling people about what you witnessed. Do you understand?"

She bites the inside of her cheek and nods her head slowly. I'm surprised how calm she is right now, but I think she's in shock.

"You will remain here as my property." I narrow my eyes, knowing she can't understand what that fully entails. "Forever."

Her head shoots up, and her eyes widen. "What about my job?"

I shake my head. "Life as you know it is over, Violet. No job anymore."

Her brow furrows. "You can't keep me as a prisoner here for the rest of my life. My friends will look for me."

I sigh heavily and pace the floor. "I have the power to make people disappear, but I don't want to kill you." I turn and glance at her. "The only way for you to live is to accept that your life is with me now. A prisoner, but you will be treated well."

She scoffs. "What kind of bullshit are you spouting, Dante?" She shakes her head. "I can either be melted in a vat of acid or forced to give up my entire life and be a prisoner with you?"

I clench my jaw. "That's right."

"I'd rather die than spend a fucking day with a murderous bastard like you."

Rage slams into me, and I charge toward her, grabbing her bound wrists and forcing her to her feet. "Careful what you wish for, Violet. Death isn't something you should wish for so quickly."

She holds my gaze, surprising me with her courage. "I

don't wish for death, but why can't I give you my word that I won't tell anyone and get on with my life?"

I laugh and let go of her wrists, letting her fall back onto the bed. "Anyone would swear what you promise in your position. I have no reason to believe you."

She doesn't say a word. "Why not kill me then?"

I turn to look at her, and my chest clenches. Violet has been in my affections for two years, and the thought of killing her is almost unthinkable. "Believe it or not, I've grown fond of you over the two years we've known each other. I'd rather not kill you, but don't for a minute believe that it's ruled out."

She visibly shudders.

I approach her again and grab the rope around her wrists. "Let me remove these." I reach for the knife at my belt and cut the bindings. Red, blistering marks are already etched into her perfect, creamy skin.

I gently run my finger across the sore skin, making her shiver. "I wish you hadn't seen what you saw tonight."

She meets my gaze as that surge of sexual tension clouds the air. Even if she looks at me with fear, the fire is buried under all the confused hatred. I'll pull it back to the surface and make sure she can't resist me. She will be mine in every sense of the word.

"I'm sorry about this, Violet." I move my hand to her face, brushing a hair away from her eye. "I didn't want to do this to you of all people."

Her throat bobs. "Then why are you doing it?"

I move my hand from her cheek, knowing that's not a

question I can answer easily. I'm the son of the richest drug lord in the world and run the operation stateside. "Because I'm a dangerous man, Violet, and I'm expected to silence any witness to my crimes." I glance back at her. "My men aren't happy that I didn't kill you right away."

She nods slowly. "I heard."

I run a hand across the back of my neck. "There are two options for you. Be my prisoner or die."

Her eyes widen at my bluntness.

"It's up to you which you prefer."

She swallows hard. "How long will I be your prisoner?"

I shake my head. "Indefinitely"

She looks like she can't believe what I'm saying. "What about my friends?" She shakes her head. "I'll never see them again?"

I clench my jaw and move even closer to her, grabbing her throat hard. "Forget about any life you once knew, Violet. There's no going back." I hold her gaze, surprised to feel that hot, fiery tension ignites between us as she stares into my eyes. She needs to know that there's no going back now. I call all of the shots, and she will learn to obey me.

Violet shudders, but I don't know if it's out of fear or desire—maybe a bit of both. I let go of her throat, and she draws a deep breath.

I turn my back on her, unable to trust myself any longer in her presence. If I'm going to meld her into my perfect submissive, then I need to do this right. "You will stay here. I'll have someone bring you new clothes and anything else you need."

My intentions aren't honorable when it comes to Violet, but I'm not cruel enough to force her to endure my presence after what she witnessed so soon. I'm twisted, but I wouldn't say I like taking a woman who doesn't want me. Violet wants me even if her desire has been tainted by her discovery of the darkness inside of me.

I'll sleep in the spare room next door until I can convince her that her only option is to submit to me.

Death isn't a choice. Normally for a witness to any of the Ortega Cartel's activity, death is the only option, but I won't allow it for her. If my father knew I were keeping Violet alive as my prisoner, he would probably kill her himself.

People think I'm a cold-hearted son of a bitch, but that's because they've not met my father. A man that is so ruthless, he shot my mother dead in front of my sister and me when I was only seven years old, and my sister was four. All because he found out she'd had an affair with her chauffeur.

My mother was unhappy after being forced to marry him in an arrangement between their families. Father was the first to be unfaithful many times, but her infidelity was disrespect that he couldn't allow. The cartel is most certainly a man's world.

I haven't seen my sister, Leticia, for ten years and don't even know if she's alive. My father sold her to one of our partner's sons as a wife and committed her to a terrible life in Columbia when she was eighteen. I can't help the twinge of sadness come over me as I remember her. We were the best of friends growing up, always there for one another—until my father broke that bond and forced me to become a man at the age of thirteen.

He made me beat her, and she never looked at me the same way again. Life in the Cartel hierarchy has been brutal and dark, and it's molded me into the man I am today. Vicious and cold-hearted. The boy I once was is buried under so much dark I know he'll never see the light of day again.

7

VIOLET

I wake early, as it's still dark outside. My heart skips a beat the moment I notice the room I'm in. Great, so it wasn't a nightmare. I've been kidnapped by the man I've fantasized about for two years. A man that turned out different than I expected.

Musicians are never good news, but Dante is so far bad. He's as dark as any man could be. I know how to pick the bad ones, even if I didn't get around to asking him out. Maybe that was a good thing in hindsight. The man is insane.

I get out of bed and walk toward the door, trying the handle again. It's still locked. Dante hasn't come back since last night, leaving me overthinking everything.

I can't understand why a man like him, dangerous enough to kidnap me for witnessing a murder, would want to keep me alive—the terrible thoughts racing through my mind about the plans he has for me fill me with dread.

The windows on the house's far wall are locked, and there are no keys in this damn room. Dante has covered every escape route, making me feel claustrophobic, something I don't normally suffer from.

A commotion from the other side of the wall startles me. I listen, holding my breath. The sound of footsteps pacing tells me there is someone in the room next door.

An older woman came up and brought me a bag of clothes, including the nightgown I'm wearing. She also brought me some food, but I couldn't stomach any of it.

I fell asleep, which I thought was going to be impossible. My heart skips a beat as I hear someone on the other side of the wall moving. I notice a door in the wall that I hadn't noticed before, and the footsteps stop in front of it.

Is this room adjoining someone else's?

I stare at the door, holding my breath. A jangle of keys on the other side of the door makes my stomach churn.

The sound of the key turning in the lock is followed by the door swinging open. Dante stands in the doorway in a pair of tight boxer briefs. The sight of his hard, chiseled muscles makes my mouth dry. I'm flooded with all-consuming heat at the sight of the dark tattoos on his chest and arms.

My racing heart quickens as he moves into the room and slams the door shut. His eyes are pinned on me intently as he walks forward. This man is a sick bastard, and I shouldn't feel anything but disgust at him entering my room in the middle of the night, half-naked.

It doesn't help that I've longed for this man for two years. The murder I witnessed him commit last night was enough to make me fear him and to know I have to resist any advance he might make. Something tells me Dante isn't someone who worries too much about consent, especially after what he did last night.

"W-what are you doing?" I ask as he continues to move closer.

It's only at that moment that I realize I'm wearing nothing but a thin nightgown the woman brought me—a sheer night-gown. His eyes are fixed on my body, and he doesn't answer.

"Dante," I say his name, hoping he will snap out of it. Instead, he keeps moving toward me, making my stomach twist with anxiety. The anxiety that I'm about to be thrown back into the nightmare I thought I'd escaped four years ago. My drunk stepdad had a thing for getting so drunk. He would come into my room and force himself on me. At the time, my mom was too sick for me to worry her about it.

I back away from him, knowing there's no escape. There is nowhere for me to go as he has me backed into a corner. My next step has my back colliding with the wall.

Dante is like a wolf stalking his prey—relentless as he continues to move closer.

"What are you doing?" I ask, surprised by the conviction in my voice.

Finally, he stops moving closer, narrowing his eyes. "What-ever the fuck I want, bonita. You belong to me now." He steps closer, sending goosebumps prickling across my skin. "You need to understand what that means," he growls, grabbing my shoulders and pinning my back hard against the wall.

"No one owns me," I say, lifting my chin in an attempt to

appear confident, even though inside I'm scared half to death. He doesn't know what I've overcome to date, I've survived that and I'm stronger. I will survive him.

A flicker of a challenge ignites in Dante's dark eyes that look almost black in the dark bedroom. "You are so wrong, nena," he says, calling me something in Spanish.

I swallow hard. "I may be your prisoner, Dante, but I'll never belong to you."

He growls softly and grabs my throat so hard it feels like he's trying to choke the life out of me. "You belonged to me long before I kidnapped you, Vi." His weight pins me against the wall as he keeps a hand on my throat, proving how little power I have.

I'm immobilized and at this monster's mercy—a monster who I'd longed for and kissed only five or six hours ago. It feels like a lifetime ago. Now, I hate him more than I can put into words. The way he snatched me as I tried to run at the club, followed by his cold stares and then this.

"Don't deny the truth. You've wanted me ever since we met." He presses his lips to my cheek, making my stomach twist. If this had happened before I'd seen him kill a man, I'd be all over him. "You still want me," he murmurs into my ear.

I shake my head and try to push him away, shocked by the sheer strength of him as he doesn't budge an inch. "Bullshit. I don't want you and never will."

He places a hand on my thigh and snakes it between my them, making me tense.

"Get the fuck off me," I shout, feeling panic rising inside

of me as the helplessness I never wanted to experience again closes in around me. "You bastard."

His fingers delve into my pussy, sending waves of unwanted pleasure through me. It's a conflicting sensation since Dante has been the object of my desires for so long. I've pictured moments like this repeatedly in my mind. I wanted him to touch me in my fantasies—I wanted him to touch me more than anything.

My mind and my body are at war as his fingers tease my soaking wet center.

"You're a fucking liar, Vi," he rumbles, continuing to slowly, softly move his fingers in and out of me. "Your pussy is soaking wet."

The conflict inside of me is so deep, but one thing I'm sure of is this is beyond wrong. I spit in Dante's face, making him stop.

His eyes flash with such rage I wonder if he's about to end it all now— rage that scares me beyond measure. He grabs my wrists hard and pins them above my head. "Are you trying to piss me off?"

I shake my head as it is all I can do. The sudden realization of the kind of man I'm fighting against hits me full force—a ruthless criminal who isn't afraid to take what he wants. By the look in his eyes, he wants me. I swallow hard, knowing that if he intends to have me, I won't be able to fight him off. It makes me sick to my stomach.

He shoves his fingers back inside of me without another word, keeping his other hand around my wrists against the wall.

"Stop it," I protest, shaking my head despite the pleasure his touch brings. "Why are you doing this?" I ask, feeling pain clutch around my heart.

It hurts me that he has so little respect for me. After two years of playful flirting followed by a kiss last night that rocked my world, this Dante isn't the man I know.

"I'm doing this because it's what you've wanted ever since we met, two years ago." He hooks his fingers inside of me in a way that drives me close to release—widening the conflict inside of me.

Dante is right. I've wanted this for so long, and finally, he's touching me the way I've dreamed. The circumstances, however, are a world away from the fantasy I've pictured.

Adrenaline pulses through me as the wrongfulness of what he's doing hits me with more force. I muster all the strength I can and manage to push him away from me.

Again, that deep and dark rage ignites in his eyes. I cross my arms over my chest, covering my exposed breasts. "Don't fucking touch me."

"Or what, señorita?" He towers over me. His presence is intimidating, but I won't let him break me.

"Or I'll kick you in the balls. Back the fuck off," I say, meeting Dante's gaze with all the courage I can muster.

It's as if my tone breaks through the dark haze that had descended on a man who I thought I knew. A man I've longed to be with for two years. He takes two steps away from me, giving me the space to breathe. My knees shake, but I try not to let him see how much his assault got to me.

He shakes his head, rubbing a hand across the back of his

neck. "I'm sorry, I…" The guilt in his eyes as clear as day. He should feel guilty.

Dante never struck me as the kind of man who would disrespect a woman the way he just did to me. However, he also never struck me as the kind of guy who could shoot another man dead in the street. I don't know him or what he is capable of at all.

"Get out," I say, holding his gaze with all my conviction.

He turns away from me and takes two steps.

I feel the tension easing away as I watch him walk toward the door. It all returns just as fast as he stops in his tracks. His back is tense as he clenches his fists.

Fuck.

Dante turns around and pins his gaze on me. "Tell me that you didn't want me before tonight," he says.

I swallow hard, wondering what he is trying to get at. "I did, Dante. Before I saw you murder a man, I wanted you with every fiber of my being."

His jaw clenches, but he doesn't walk toward me. "And now?"

I bite my bottom lip, knowing a part of me still does want to feel his touch, his lips and all of him on me—a very small part of me. "Now, I can't stand the thought of you touching me." I shake my head. "I don't know you at all."

He moves toward me slowly, holding his hands up slightly as if in surrender. "I'm sorry for touching you like that." He shakes his head. "I saw you half-naked, and my resolve snapped." He stops a few steps away from me. "I'm the same man, Violet. The same man you've watched sing and play guitar for two years."

Bullshit.

"No, the man I thought I knew would never kill a guy or put his hands on me when I asked him to stop." My chest aches as I utter those words. "You are not the man I've fantasized about for two years."

His eyes narrow. "You will come around to the idea of being mine, Vi." He turns his back on me again and walks away. "It's your only choice."

The dark tone of his voice makes me shiver. He doesn't look back this time, marching straight through the open door and slamming it hard.

The slam of the door doesn't even make me jump, as I'm too numb.

I don't know what time it is as there's no clock in this room. All I know is there is no way I'm going to sleep after what just happened. I walk to a small armchair in the corner of the room and sit on it, curling my legs up into my chest.

The tears I couldn't shed before flood down my face as I sob over what has happened. My world has been flipped upside down in a matter of hours, and it feels like nothing will ever be right again.

8

DANTE

I sit at my desk, reading a contract with a building contractor for a new bar we are planning in Queens. A bar that will help pick up the slack when it comes to laundering our money. It's coming in quicker than ever, and our current operations can't handle it. The Irish have been trying to block us every fucking step we make, using some planning office ties. Finally, we've got approval to build.

The next time that asshole, Devlin Murphy, decides to move against me, I'm going to come at him with all I've got. I won't rest until he's buried six feet under. My father has put pressure on me to up my game, or he will come and visit me. I haven't seen him in six years, and I don't want to. It's best for all of us that we keep him happy. A visit from him is always bad news.

Someone knocks at my door.

"Come in," I say.

Javier opens the door and stands in front of my desk. "Boss, we've got a problem."

If it's not one problem it's another. "What is it?"

He sits in the chair opposite me, shaking his head. "Salvador thinks that the Álvaro cartel took out Miguel, and there is talk of a gang war erupting on New York soil between our guys and his."

Salvador is one of our distributors here in New York City. "Fuck," I say, standing and pacing the floor. "I forgot how close Miguel was to Salvador. The guy disrespected me, and I couldn't let it slide." I glance at my lugarteniente. "Get me a meeting set up with Salvador. I need to end this before it even starts."

Javier nods. "I'm already ahead of you, boss. He's coming to meet us here for lunch today."

I grit my teeth, as I'd planned to have lunch with Violet. I need to try to repair the damage I did two mornings ago. When I saw her out of her bed in a sheer nightgown, my self-control snapped. I couldn't help myself, and I only made Violet's dislike for me grow.

Vi is my slave. She is here to do with what I want, but I think I pushed her too quickly. It's no fun if the woman I want doesn't enjoy my advances, and that takes patience when dealing with a woman taken against her will.

Every rule I threw out the window that morning. I couldn't sleep, so I decided to check on the woman haunting my thoughts, assuming she'd be asleep. I did not expect to see her out of bed almost naked in a sheer, cream slip that left nothing to the imagination.

I stand from my desk and walk over to the dresser where my rum is. I pour myself a glass, glancing at Javier. "Do you want one?"

He shakes his head, brow furrowed. If he's confused as to why I'm drinking at ten o'clock in the morning, he doesn't voice his concern—he wouldn't dare.

"What time is Salvador arriving?" I ask, trying to keep my mind off of the encounter with Violet.

Her perfect, firm breasts were entirely visible, and I haven't been able to erase that image ever since. I don't know what kind of reception to expect when I approach her again. She's been locked in the adjoining room to mine.

Things got dark way too quickly, and that darkness snuffed out any desire she used to look at me with. I know that it isn't gone, though. An attraction that deep and long developed doesn't disappear overnight.

Confinement, even for a couple of days, can either break someone's resolve or make it. Violet strikes me as a strong woman. The way she pushed me off of her was impressive, and she didn't cower at my rage.

Javier clears his throat. "He'll be here at twelve-thirty." There's a moment of awkward, tense silence. "What did you do with the bartender from El Torero?"

I meet his gaze, feeling angry at being questioned about Violet at all. "She's locked away in the room adjoining mine. Why?"

He shrugs. "Carlos has been asking questions."

I knock back the rest of the rum, slamming my tumbler on

the desk. "That bastard doesn't get to ask questions. Have you asked him for the money he owes?"

Javier nods. "Yes, he asked for a one week extension." He shrugs. "I've let him have it as long as he makes the payment in a week."

Motherfucker.

"You should have checked with me first. He's been taking liberties with us too much lately. If he doesn't pay on time, then a visit will be in order." I shake my head. "Tell him that Violet is no longer his concern. Tell him she belongs to The Ortega Cartel, and if he has a problem, he can come and see me about it."

"Sure thing, boss." He looks at me in a way that tells me something is on his mind. I've known him since we were kids, and I know that look too well.

"What is it, Javier?"

He swallows. "I wondered why you haven't killed Violet yet."

I glare at my lugarteniente, wondering where he got the balls to question me on this. "Javier, is it any of your business what I do with her?"

Javier shakes his head. "No, but I don't want to leave any loose ends. Violet is a loose end. Also, have you forgotten about your upcoming wedding?"

Bastard.

I can't believe he has brought Rosa into this. My father has arranged my marriage to a woman I haven't met. I've been putting it off for exactly one year and a half. He has been increasing the pressure on me to visit Mexico and marry her.

"Rosa won't be my wife. I don't care what my father says. Arranged marriages don't fucking work."

Javier nods. "I agree, boss, but your father wants an heir to the family business. You are his only son."

I crack my neck and glare at my friend. "Have you been in touch with him?"

He nods. "He sent word to me a week ago, asking me to convince you to come to Mexico within two months and marry her. He said if I fail, he will be paying you a visit himself."

Rage floods me at only now being told this. "You only thought to mention this once I asked you?"

"He asked in the letter not to mention that he was pushing. I'm sorry, jefe."

I slam my fist against the desk. "You work for me, Javier. Not that fucking bastard." I feel the rage building inside of me as I walk around the desk and tower over his chair. "Violet is locked in my home and isn't getting out. Don't fucking worry about her. She's mine."

His eyes widen at the proclamation that I own her—a possessiveness that is uncharacteristic. My father constantly owned women, but I've always steered clear from enslaving anyone, women or men.

Javier holds his hands up. "Of course, I'm sorry." He stands. "If that is all, I'll make preparations for Salvador's arrival."

I nod, thankful that he knows when to give it a rest. "Yes, that is all." If it had been Ric having this same conversation, it would have come to blows. When it comes to Violet, he should never bring her up again.

She's mine even if she won't accept it yet. I'll give her time to fall back in love with the real me—failure is not an option.

Javier leaves my office, shutting the door softly behind him. It looks like I'm going to have to wait until tonight to see how two days captivity has affected Violet.

My staff members are under orders to keep that door locked, except Angela. She is the only person allowed to take her food irregularly in an attempt to break her resolve. There's no entertainment inside that room, not even a clock to keep track of time.

Our *prior* relationship at the club has to be squashed. Violet needs to know her position here. A prisoner in a plush, fancy prison who answers to me and me alone. I know that my infatuation with her is a complication—feelings that never should have arisen between us are there.

My early morning visit to her room was a taster of what she has to expect. I want her in a primal way, and I will get what I want. Her resistance wasn't surprising as I was a fucking asshole. The moment I set eyes on her firm breasts and hard nipples under that slip, I lost my senses.

All the blood in my body rushed south, and I was not thinking with my brain. I was thinking with my rock-hard cock that wanted nothing more than to be buried deep inside her.

Violet will have to learn to want me, desire me, and love me. Something tells me that's going to be one of my most difficult challenges yet, but it's one that I look forward to.

THE DINING TABLE is laid out with a huge amount of food, ready for Salvador's arrival. I sit at one end, waiting patiently. All the while, I can't stop my mind from wandering onto Violet. I need to focus if I'm going to get through this without pissing off our best distributor.

Salvador is Miguel's cousin—the man I shot dead and dissolved in a vat of acid only three nights ago.

He won't be happy when I tell him the truth, but Salvador knows how things work. A dealer can't approach me—not ever. It's the rules. I'm the top of the fucking food chain here in New York, and that stupid son of a bitch thought it wise to approach me in a back alley.

It proves that he was the kind of guy that wouldn't have survived on the streets anyway. Javier opens the door to the dining room and leads Salvador inside. I don't stand as it's custom to remain seated if you are the boss.

"Welcome, Salvador," I say, giving him a nod. "Take a seat."

Salvador looks uneasy and on edge, which I'd expect. It's not every day a distributor of mine gets invited to my home, but this is a courtesy that was necessary after what I did to his family member.

"Thank you, sir." He takes a seat, sitting forward.

"Relax, Salvador. There is nothing to be on edge about."

He does relax slightly and sits back. "I see, so why the invite if you don't mind me asking, sir?"

I meet Javier's gaze, and he gives me a nod. "I heard you

intend to wage war against Álvaro cartel?" A war that nobody wants. If war breaks out here, it breaks out much worse south of the fucking border, and I'd be answering to my father.

"They killed my cousin, Miguel."

I shake my head. "Who told you that?"

Salvador bites his lip. "An informant."

"Well, you should sack that fucking informant. I killed Miguel." I hold his gaze and feel nothing. Even as the grief is evident in Salvador's eyes, I feel no regret for taking that man's life.

His brow furrows. "What?"

I glance at Javier, wanting him to explain.

Javier sets his hands on the table in front of him. "Miguel approached Dante in a back alley and disrespected him. He had no choice but to end him for his blatant disregard for the rules of our operation."

The rage in Salvador's eyes is evident, but I know he won't lash out—not unless he wants to end up in the same vat of acid as his cousin. "I see." He glances down at his clenched fists. "I assume we won't be getting his body back?"

Javier shakes his head. "Not possible."

The tension in the air is so high you could slice through it with a knife.

"I assume we won't have any problems. You of all people know that the cartel has to run like clockwork and insubordinate dealers have to be dealt with swiftly, no matter who they are or who they are related to," I say.

Salvador nods. "Of course."

The fear that I incite in my men is intoxicating. They

wouldn't dare question me. My father's brutal reputation rubbed off on me, and they expect the same kind of brutality, even if I'm not quite as bad as him. I do what I have to do to survive as the leader of our family business.

I clap my hands. "Perfect. Now, let's eat." I glance at Salvador. "We don't want all this food that Paula spent so much time preparing to go to waste, do we?"

Salvador swallows hard and shakes his head, spooning food onto his plate. It used to amuse me how much fear I inspire, but now it's become a natural part of my life. I grab myself some shrimp and bean chili, tucking in. There will be more than enough food leftover tonight, and I'll get Paula to serve it back up for Violet and me.

Angela is under instructions to get her ready. I picked out her dress, and she will be brought down to the dining room at seven o'clock.

An awkward silence falls between the three of us until Javier speaks. "Salvador how is your wife?"

Salvador takes the question as a threat, which knowing Javier was not the intention. "S-she is well. Pregnant with our first child." He glances nervously at me, but I don't soften my gaze.

"Boy or girl?" I ask.

He swallows hard. "A boy. She is due in two months."

I hold my wine glass up. "Congratulations. Another warrior for the Ortega Cartel, I hope?"

He nods. "Of course, sir. He will be brought up as strong and loyal as me."

I nod, satisfied by his answer. Salvador is right about that.

He's as loyal as they come, and that's why I knew I could tell him the truth about his cousin. A war between the two cartels has to be avoided on this side of the border at all costs. I won't have my father's wrath come down on me for a war that could be so easily avoided.

9

VIOLET

I'm going out of my mind locked in this room. All I know is today is the second day I've been trapped, but it feels like I've been in here a lifetime. I found a piece of paper and pen in the dresser, and I am noting down the number of nights to keep track.

The woman who comes to bring me food once a day won't say a word to me. She ignores every question I ask her and walks out without even a goodbye. I didn't eat the first day, but today the hunger won, and I devoured the surprisingly delicious tacos that she brought up to me.

I felt ashamed that I couldn't hold out longer, as I had no intention of taking anything Dante offered me. The love and desire I once held for him is entirely gone after the way he treated me. I'm thankful he hasn't returned, but I know it's only a matter of time.

Footsteps stop outside my room and I assume it's around

about lunch time as that's when Angela brings me one meal for the day. She opens the door, but I'm surprised to see she's not holding a tray like she usually is. Instead, she has a garment bag over her arm.

"You will be dining with Mr. Ortega this evening. He has instructed that you wear this." She signals to the garment bag, shutting the door and hanging it on the back. "I believe you have makeup in the supplies I bought you on the first night, don't you?"

I nod, a little surprised that she's actually talking to me.

"Well, use some. You look a mess, wash and brush your hair." She shakes her head. "Mr. Ortega doesn't want to eat dinner with a vagrant. I will come and get you at ten to seven to ensure you are at dinner on time."

I sigh heavily. "How am I supposed to know when that is if I don't have a clock?"

She gives me an irritated glare. "You've got just under six hours, so make sure you are ready early." She glances around the room. "It's not like you have anything else to do."

I narrow my eyes at her. "What if I don't want to have dinner with Mr. Ortega." It feels so weird calling him that—so formal.

She glares at me. "You don't have a say in the matter. Be ready or there will be consequences." She sets a shoe box she was holding in her hand down on the floor, before opening the door. "Don't be late, whatever you do," she adds, before storming out of the room and slamming the door with a thud.

The jangle of keys follows as she locks the door. Those are the first words she's ever said to me and she is as much of a bitch as I expected her to be. Stuck up housekeeper who thinks she's better than everyone around her. I know her type.

I get up off the edge of the bed and approach the door, wondering what kind of dress Dante wants me to wear. The label on the garment bag is some fancy boutique in Manhattan I've never heard of. I pull down the zipper to reveal a golden maxi dress with slit from thigh down and very low neckline.

Exactly the kind of thing I'd expect him to want me to wear after he tried to make a move on me without my consent. The man is a pig. My stomach churns at the thought of having to sit down opposite him at dinner and play nice. If Dante expects me to act as if nothing is wrong, then he is in for a surprise.

I sigh heavily and peel off the t-shirt and pants I'm wearing, before heading to the bathroom. The woman is right that I haven't got anything better to do than get ready for tonight. I'll start with a long hot soak in the bath. All I wish is that I had my damn kindle to at least read something.

If Dante thinks he can break me by isolating me and boring me out of my mind, he will have to step up his game. I turn the faucet on the bath on and wait for it to warm up. Once it's warm I put the stopper in followed by some essential bath oils that smell amazing.

I dip my toes in as it fills up, making sure it's not too hot. The bath fills up quickly and I turn the faucet off, climbing inside. I sigh as my muscles relax in the warm water and I shut my eyes. This is the first time I've washed since I was kidnapped, feeling too paralyzed with shock to do anything.

I swallow hard as my clit reacts to the warmth and begins to throb. Instantly the memory of Dante's fingers moving in and out of me hits me and I grit my teeth. It was fucking wrong because I told him no, and yet, it was one of the most intoxicating experiences of my life. His hard body pressing against me and making it impossible for me to move was weirdly arousing.

I slip my fingers between my thighs and slowly move them in and out, imagining him doing it again. It's wrong, but I can't understand why it felt so right. He wants me so badly that he couldn't stop himself—it makes me feel more desired than I've ever felt before.

I shut my eyes as I think about Dante's hands all over me. Despite the circumstances, the reality of his touch far outweighed the fantasy. I hate him but want him all at the same time. It's the oddest sensation ever. I continue to touch myself, moaning and writhing under the water as I strum myself closer and closer to release.

My head rests back against the edge of the tub and I can't stop myself from crying out his name. The image of him in those tight boxer briefs is all I can see in my mind. I shake from the force of one of the best orgasms I've ever had, thinking about Dante.

Dinner with him is a disaster waiting to happen if I can't get a handle on my questionable desires.

I FIX my hair in the mirror one last time. At least, I think it will be the last time. It's impossible to gauge time when you don't have a fucking clock.

I've never looked this fancy in all my life. The dress is unbelievably beautiful. All I'm worried about is what Dante is going to expect from me. I won't be his toy or plaything.

I glance in the mirror again. Life has a way of taking turns you never see coming, and this is the biggest turn I've ever encountered. Dante kissed me Friday night. For the first time, we both crossed that line and gave in to the pull of desire we both felt. Less than half an hour later, I see that same man commit a murder and then kidnap me for it.

It was over before it started. The same may well go for my life. I'm only twenty-four years old, and I haven't gotten around to any of the things I wanted to do before I die.

The jangle of keys at the door makes my heart rate accelerate. Maybe I'm getting the hang of keeping time without a watch. The past six hours have gone by faster than I expected, and I think it's because I never wanted this moment to come.

When you want time to slow down, it speeds up and vice versa. The lady stands in the doorway. "I hope you are—" She stops when she sees me, eyes wide. "You scrub up well," she says.

I take that as a compliment since this woman has only been cold to me up to now. "Thanks."

She nods. "Come on. We want you down in the dining room before Mr. Ortega."

The mention of Dante makes my stomach churn again. I

should feel like a princess in this dress, but I feel like a piece of meat instead—prepared and ready for that man to feast on.

Following after her into the corridor, I don't argue as it's my first glimpse of freedom from that room in two days. As we walk down the corridor, I pay attention. If I ever get a chance to escape, I'm going to take it without hesitation.

She leads me to the top of a sweeping staircase—not the staircase we used when Dante brought me in here. It's interesting to know there are two.

I look down into the hallway, and instantly my eyes meet Dante's. I hate the way my heart skips a beat the moment our gazes collide. It seems that despite the way he treated me the other morning, my desire for him isn't entirely snuffed out. The look in his eyes is one of pure, burning hunger—hunger for me.

He looks darkly beautiful in a form-fitting suit that only makes him look more appealing. I've only ever seen him in a shirt and leather jacket—casual. In formal wear, he's even more attractive, which I didn't believe possible.

Remember who he is and what he does.

In a fairy tale, I'd be a princess walking to join my prince. He sure as hell looks the part. Instead, I'm going to join the devil. A man so dark I don't think I have a full grasp of what he's capable of or who he is yet.

The desire in his eyes increases as they move down my body and back up to my face again. I can't help the smirk that twists onto my lips at the way he adjusts his pants. He may be an asshole for touching me when I told him to stop in my room, but I can't help feeling powerful suddenly that I have such an effect on him. An effect he doesn't seem to be able to control.

"Good evening, señorita," Dante says, taking my hand softly and pressing his lips to the back of it.

I hate the shiver that runs from the tip of my fingers down my spine. "Evening," I say, pulling my hand away quickly.

There's a flash of irritation in his eyes as his jaw clenches. He glances at the woman who brought me here. "That will be all, Angela."

She nods at him and walks away, leaving us alone.

Dante stares at me with an intensity that both scares and excites me. I hate that he still has the power to excite me. "Shall we?" he asks, holding out his arm for me to take.

Part of me wants to take it, but I know I shouldn't. After what happened the other morning, we need to keep touching to a minimum.

I swallow hard and cross my arms over my chest. "Sure, lead the way."

He clenches his jaw, walking ahead of me down a corridor off the main entrance hall. I follow behind him cautiously. My stomach twists with anxiety as I keep my attention focused on Dante's tense form.

At the bar, Dante was always so cool and calm. It's almost impossible to accept the same man walks in front of me. He stops in front of a door and opens it. I follow him into what looks to be an office with a small, intimate table set out in the center lit with candles.

It's too romantic a setting for the occasion. If Dante thinks he can seduce me after the shit he pulled, then he's wrong.

Everything about this situation is fucked up. He's dressing me up in a dress, and he's in a suit, bringing me to a dimly lit room with dinner. The man kidnapped me and has had me locked in a room for two days.

Two years of fantasizing about the man sitting opposite me will make saying no to him far more difficult. I wouldn't admit it out loud to anyone, but I am addicted to his dominance. The way he took what he wanted from me that morning in my room turned me on, which makes no sense.

I shouldn't want a man that doesn't respect my wishes, but there's no denying the truth. Dante is the villain of my story. The problem is I've always had a weakness for villains that know exactly what they want and who aren't afraid to take it.

10

DANTE

*V*iolet sits in silence at the other end of the table. The dining room seemed too large for the two of us, especially since I want to break down the walls she's erected. My office is still a large and substantial room, but more intimate.

I didn't miss the whisper of a smirk on her lips at the look I gave her when I saw her walk down those sweeping steps in the dress I picked out. I knew she'd look amazing, but I wasn't quite prepared for how stunning she looks.

Beautiful doesn't go far enough to describe the way she looks tonight. I'm not sure there is a word in the English or Spanish language that can do her justice. An angel walked down those steps sent straight from heaven into the devil's lair.

"Wine?" I ask, holding up a five-hundred-dollar bottle of red wine—I got Leo to pick out one of our better bottles in the wine cellar. I'm not that into wine, but I always see Violet sipping a glass of red after a shift.

She shrugs. "Sure."

I stand from my seat and walk over to her side, purposely standing behind her to see what kind of reaction I get.

She tenses—no doubt remembering what I did to her that morning. It was a mistake—a mistake that is going to make seducing my princess harder. Her walls are up, but maybe after a bottle or two of wine, she'll start to relax. I need to make her remember why she wanted me in the first place. I'm still the same man I always was.

I pour her a glass before returning to my seat and pouring myself a glass.

She brings it to her lips and slowly sips it. The movement is so fucking seductive, but I don't think she means it to be. Two years of wanting a woman can make everything she does sexy as hell. A few moments of silence follow as she returns the glass to the table and meets my gaze.

"How do you like it?" I ask.

Her tongue darts out over her lips, making my cock harden in my pants. The image of me plowing every inch of it into her throat until she can hardly breathe floods into my mind.

"It's good and ridiculously expensive."

I nod. "You are worth it, señorita."

Her brow furrows. "Cut the crap, Dante. What is this dinner all about?"

Her no-bullshit attitude only makes me want her more. "You've been locked in that room for two days. I thought you might want some time out of there." I lift my glass to my lips, holding her gaze over the rim as I take a sip. "I want to discuss with you what your options are."

She shifts uncomfortably in her chair. "I didn't think I had any options. I'm your prisoner, and that's all there is to it."

Violet is smart, and she knows what I want from her. She's just too scared to face it.

"Not exactly, you do have options." I shake my head. "Eat some food, and we will talk about it after. You must be hungry."

There is a flash of anger in her stunning crystal blue eyes as I'm the one who has kept her hungry so that she couldn't resist eating with me. She bites her bottom lip as if deciding whether or not to be stubborn and refuse to eat. In the end, she reluctantly grabs some burritos and shrimp.

I can't help but smile.

She's a survivor that's for sure. No matter how much you hate your captor, if they offer you a free for all on food, take it. You don't know when your next meal will be.

I grab a couple of tacos and start to eat, but I'm not hungry. My mind is on an entirely different meal I want to feast on—Violet. It's impossible to stop the dirty fucking thoughts flooding my mind.

Violet eats frantically, desperately stuffing food into her mouth as if she is starving. I know she hasn't eaten since lunchtime yesterday. "Slow down, nena. It's not going anywhere, and if you fill up on the entree, you won't have space for dessert."

She swallows hard and nods. "What does nena mean?" she asks tentatively.

I smile at her question, knowing the answer will make her uncomfortable. "Its English equivalent would be baby girl." I hold her gaze, noticing the flash of desire that enters her eyes.

Her cheeks redden, and she looks down at her plate, breaking our eye contact. The sexual tension between us is always there, even after everything I've done. It's raw and palpable and impossible to deny.

"Do you like the food?" I ask.

She looks up again. "It's fine, not as good as Enrique's food, though."

I chuckle at that. "No, I have to agree with you. Maybe I should get a new cook."

She doesn't say anything, continuing to eat in silence. Even though she is ravenous, she eats elegantly—the kind of woman who was made to be by my side at special events. My power in this city gives me invites to all sorts of galas and events that I rarely attend. Perhaps with Violet on my arm, I'd feel more inclined to go. I don't fit in alone.

"Tell me, princess, where are you from originally?" I ask, trying to learn more about the woman I've set my sights on for so long.

She looks up, a little surprised by the question. "I'm from Florida."

I nod in reply. "What brought you to New York?"

Violet tips the rest of the wine in her glass down her throat. "My stepdad was an asshole, and I wanted to get as far away from him as physically possible." She looks uncomfortable mentioning her stepdad.

"What of your mother?" I ask.

A flash of sorrow enters her eyes. "She died of cancer six years ago."

The twinge of compassion that ignites inside of me shocks me, as part of me wants to console her.

I ignore it. "I'm sorry to hear that."

Violet shrugs. "Life sucks. My real dad died when I was three years old fighting in the military."

My princess has sure known sorrow in her life from the sounds of it. A true survivor. "Why did you want to get away from your stepdad?"

She tenses and shakes her head. "I think that's enough questions about me."

I narrow my eyes. "I get to decide when I've asked enough questions, Vi." I stand and walk toward her, holding the bottle of red wine. Violet tenses as I lean over to fill her glass up. "However, I will give you a break." She relaxes when she realizes the only reason that I crossed over her side of the table was to fill her glass.

Her wine glass empties quickly again as we talk about the band. I keep filling her up, and each time I come over to her side of the table, she tenses a little less. Her inhibitions are slowly melting away with each glass.

"I don't think I've told you yet, señorita, but you look more beautiful than any woman I've ever seen." I hold her gaze, assuming that she will break the eye contact and refuse my compliment.

Her tongue darts out nervously over her bottom lip. "You don't look bad yourself."

Heat floods every vein in my body, and I can feel more

blood rushing south. If she doesn't want me to make a move, she's going about this the wrong way. My cock is as hard as stone as I try to adjust myself in my pants. "Careful, princess. I'm as hard as a rock for you." I hold her gaze, surprised when she doesn't break it.

There is a desire in her eyes—desire that drives me wild.

I tilt my head to the side. "Unless you want me hard?" I raise a brow. "Do you want to suck daddy's cock, princess?"

Her eyes widen slightly as not many American women are into the daddy kink. It's more common in my culture. I love the dominance it gives me when a woman calls me that, but I'm not sure Violet would be so inclined to do so.

She shakes her head. "No." There's something in her eyes, though, a challenging look that tells me she wants me to over-step the boundary again. Perhaps she liked being touched the way I touched her that morning. She was soaking wet for me.

"If I came over there right now and shoved my fingers in your tight little pussy, would I find you are soaking wet for me, again?"

She draws in a sharp intake of breath and shuffles in the chair uncomfortably. Her cheeks grow an even deeper red. "No, you would not," she says.

I smirk at her. "Something tells me that you are lying to me, princess." I wave my hand in the air. "Never mind that. Let us discuss your options."

"Options?" she says, flustered as if she doesn't remember why I invited her to dinner in the first place.

I nod. "Yes, you witnessed me kill a man, which means you can never be free again."

Her face pales, and she glances down at her plate. "Yeah, I know."

I hate the twinge of sadness that tugs at my chest, seeing her so broken. Violet was always fiery and passionate—it's one of the reasons I've wanted her for so long. "That being said, you do have a choice." I run a hand across the back of my neck. "If you can see yourself being happy by my side, I will treat you like a fucking queen—my queen"

"By your side?" she asks, sounding a little dumbfounded.

I nod. "My woman. Mine to kiss. Mine to fuck when I want."

Her eyes widen. "So, a whore?"

I slam my hand down on the table as the term angers me greatly. "No. You would be my wife, Violet. You would provide me with children and be mine."

She shakes her head. "And, if I refuse?"

I grit my teeth, knowing that the answer to that is too complicated to contend with right now. Violet means too much for me to let her go. There's no chance I could ever kill her, which means she either has to accept my job offer or I'd be forced to send her down to Mexico to the mercy of my father. Although, I'm not entirely sure I could do that either.

"Your fate would rest in my father's hands if you refuse the offer I'm about to give you. Raúl Ortega is renowned for being brutal and vicious beyond anything you could ever imagine." I sigh heavily. "I can't hurt you, Violet. The rules of our world are simple—all witnesses to our crimes die."

"Then kill me." Her hands shake as she utters those words. Words that cut me deeper than I expect.

"You'd rather die than be my wife?" I ask.

She meets my gaze with a conviction that shocks me. "I'd rather have the choice to decide my fate. I won't marry a man I don't want to marry and be unhappy for the rest of my life."

I knew this would be a tough sell, especially to a woman so headstrong as Violet. The promise of life isn't enough to tempt her into my arms.

"I'll prove to you that I can make you happy, Violet."

She shakes her head. "How? By touching me when I tell you to stop?" she asks, her voice cracking slightly.

"No. You are right. I crossed a line." I swallow hard. "I saw you half-naked, and I couldn't think straight. You drive me wild, princess."

Violet tucks her hair behind her ear, lifting her chin. "How exactly do you propose to prove to me you can make me happy?" The confidence in her gaze is alluring.

"My proposal to you goes against all the rules of my father's Cartel. However, I don't want you dead, Violet." I stand and approach her, taking her hand in mine. "Stand."

She stands and doesn't pull her hand away.

"I propose that you sign a contractual agreement and non-disclosure agreement also." I nod toward the coffee table to one side. "The agreements are over there. The non-disclosure agreement states that you will never speak of what you saw me do to anyone."

Violet nods. "I have no intention of—"

I hold my hand up as promises that she wouldn't tell anyone anyway mean nothing. "The contract states that for two months, you will be mine—my fiancé for that time. It also states that if you still don't want to marry me after those two months, I will free you from the engagement. You will be free." I shrug. "Well, as free as you can be."

She raises a brow. "And, if I don't want to marry you after two months, I'm going to be killed by your father?"

I clench my jaw, knowing it's a shit fucking agreement for her. "I'll offer you a position of employment in my home. You will be given a very generous wage and be free to a certain extent. I will only offer this to you as a courtesy. However, if there is any sign that you might betray me, then yes, you will answer to my father."

I can see her thinking about everything I'm saying. "What exactly do you mean I will be yours for two months?"

I can't help but smirk at her innocent question. I'm going to have Violet one way or another. The best option is she agrees to my proposal. "It's all in the contract. Why don't you take your glass of wine over there and read it?"

She nods and takes her glass from the table, walking elegantly over to the coffee table and grabbing the contract. I watch her sink onto the sofa.

The contract is generous to her if she doesn't want to marry me. She will be paid very well to work in my home. Although she will never get her old life back, she will have a semblance of a life. However, I know that won't be an issue. Two months is enough time to get her hooked on me, and she'll never want to leave by the time I'm through with her.

I join her on the sofa, sitting at enough distance not to make her uncomfortable. Her cheeks are pink and eyes wide as she reads what it means to sign that contract. She will essentially be my wife during that time and expected to be mine in every sense of the word.

The contract isn't long, but it's clear what I want from her. When she's finished, she places the paperwork on the table and looks me in the eye. There's a hatred in her eyes that I've never seen before as she glares at me.

"You expect me to fuck my way out of this?" she asks, the rage in her voice is clear.

I shrug. "I expect you to give my proposal a chance and live with me as my fiancé for two months."

"It's a lot to think about." She lifts her wine glass to her lips and knocks back the rest of her fifth glass. "Why two months?"

"Two months is all I have until my father is going to insist that I marry some Mexican drug dealer's daughter I've never met."

Violet's eyes widen. "You're engaged?"

"I never agreed to the engagement." I shake my head. "That's not the point. Will you sign?"

Violet's eyes widen. "You want an answer right now?"

I knock back my glass of rum, since I switched over after the first glass of red wine. "Yes. It's not that hard, is it?"

She stares back at me with a bewildered look on her face. A look that tells me she has no idea whether to agree or not to the contract terms. Finally, she shakes her head. "No, I will sign the contract."

"Perfect." I set the pen in her hand. "Sign it now."

She narrows her eyes at me. "And, then what?"

The anger in her eyes only stirs that dark, hot need inside

of me. My cock is hard in my pants as I hold her gaze. "Then I'll show you what you've been missing, Vi."

She shakes her head. "If I agree to this, we go at my pace. Do you understand?"

I shake my head and lean closer to her, wrapping my fingers softly around her throat. "No, princess. I'm in charge, and we will go at my pace."

Her lip trembles slightly—the only sign that she's affected by my dominance. I wonder if she's going to put up a fight as she stares into my eyes for a few beats. Instead, she nods and signs the contracts.

Violet is finely mine, and I can't wait to own her entirely—body, soul, and mind will be mine well before the two months are up.

11

VIOLET

I think I signed myself away to the devil. The look in Dante's eyes once I'd signed the contract was cruel. He owns me now for two months. It's a struggle to work out whether I want him or hate him.

Dante sets his hand on my exposed leg, and every hair on my body stands on end. I shiver, wishing that his touch didn't have any effect on me.

I yawn. "I'm really tired," I say, hoping that he will get the gist.

He chuckles. "Tired from lying around in a room for two days doing nothing?"

I cross my arms over my chest. "And who's fault was that? You chucked me in there and locked the door."

Dante smirks at me, and it makes my blood boil. The guy is cocky as hell. I found it attractive when he was a self-assured guitarist in a band, but now it's irritating because he's holding me here against my will.

He inches his fingers higher up my leg, moving to my thigh and pressing his fingertips hard into my skin. "I will be in your bed tonight."

"In your dreams," I spit.

He grabs a handful of my hair and yanks my head back, forcing me to look into his dark, soulless eyes roughly. "Don't play games with me, Vi. You read the contract."

My stomach twists as I did read the contract—a contract that made my obligations clear. It was also my only way out of this with any semblance of a life. A promised salary five times what I earn as a waitress to work in his home seemed like a good idea, but I think I underestimated tolerating Dante doing what he wants with me for two months.

"Yes, I read it." I swallow hard. "Let go of my hair."

He presses his lips to the edge of my jaw. "Or what?"

My jaw clenches, and I glare at him with a burning hatred. He knows all too well that there is nothing I can do to stop him. I'm helpless, and it's one of the most gut-wrenching sensations I've experienced in so long. All my life, I've fought to be in control of every aspect of it. From a young age, I was forced to take care of myself. Dante has managed to under-mine my independence in less than a week, leaving me weak and pathetic.

"That's what I thought, princess." He murmurs, slipping his hand down the front of my dress and cupping one of my breasts. Dante flicks my already hard nipple, making me gasp.

"Dante. I told you, I'm tired." I hold his gaze, trying to

make him believe I don't want this. Perhaps I'm trying to convince myself a little too. It's almost impossible to maintain any self-control when a man I've spent countless nights fantasizing about is touching me like this, even if he is a criminal who I should be terrified of.

At first, I was terrified. This man is a killer.

He licks a path up the column of my neck, sending my mind reeling. The pleasure from his touch is too much to resist. I feel myself relax into his arms, submitting to him as he kisses every exposed area of skin. "You are so fucking beautiful," he says, grabbing the right strap of my dress and pulling it down. "I need to see every inch of you."

I quiver as he exposes my right breast first, groaning softly. The look in his eyes is hungry and desperate as if he's ready to ravage me like the monster he is. I know it's sick that I find this dark, beastly side of him a turn on.

He covers my hard nipple with his mouth and sucks on it hungrily, sending waves of pleasure cresting through me. His hand slides my left dress strap down, freeing my other breast.

I moan as he rolls my hard nipple between his finger and thumb, driving me wild. "Dante," I breathe his name, feeling overcome by hot, frantic desire.

He stops, flashing me the sexiest smile I've ever seen. "Yes, princess?"

I bite my tongue, realizing that he has turned me into a needy mess within minutes, and I want to beg him to continue. "Let's go upstairs."

He tilts his head slightly, intrigued by my suggestion. "Can't wait to get me into bed, baby girl?"

I shake my head. "No, I don't feel comfortable here." Any of Dante's staff could walk in at any moment and see me half-naked.

"No one is going to walk in."

I shrug. "I'd be more comfortable in my room."

He sighs and nods. "Whatever you want, princess." He quickly slips my dress back up and lifts me into his arms as if I weigh nothing.

"I can walk, you know." I glare at him, irritated that he's taking everything from me, even my freedom to walk.

"Relax and enjoy the ride." He carries me out of the room past Angela, the lady bringing me food and supplies. Her eyes widen as she sees me in his arms.

I don't hold onto him, feeling uncomfortable about the whole Prince Charming act. The guy is a killer and not a Prince. He opens the door to my room with one hand and carries me to the bed, gently placing me on it.

It's odd that I feel safe once back in this room—it may be my prison, but it's also my refuge.

Dante unbuttons his shirt without saying anything, tossing it on the floor casually. His shoes go next, followed by his pants. When he turns back around, he's only wearing a pair of tight briefs that leave nothing to the imagination. He's hard and, from the looks of it, huge.

"Get out of that dress now, princess. I want to see every inch of you." The heat in his eyes is enough to melt me. For a few moments, I stand there staring at his beautiful body. The last time I saw him like this, it was dark, and I couldn't truly admire the tattoos scaling over his skin and how muscular he is.

He starts to walk toward me. "Did you hear me?"

I nod, tearing my eyes away from him and slipping out of my dress. It drops to the floor in a pool around my ankles, leaving me standing in only a skimpy black thong. When I look back up, Dante is already heading toward me with a hunger in his eyes that scares me and excites me all at the same time. This man is a ruthless killer, but he's also the man I've pictured in this exact scenario thousands of times.

He collides with me, capturing my lips hard. I feel his tongue against them, demanding entrance. As his tongue tangles with mine, I feel all reasoning escape me and pure pleasure course through my very being.

I feel the fabric of my skimpy thong soaking wet between my thighs. I bite my lip, trying to stop the moan on the tip of my tongue. Dante moves his hands to my breasts, cupping them. It's all it takes for me to lose control of what restrain I have as I moan loudly.

He groans against my skin and leans down to suck my nipples into his mouth, lavishing attention on each one. Slowly, he kisses a path down my tummy before stopping just above my pussy. My thighs quiver in anticipation.

Dante doesn't move lower, teasing me as he kisses a path back to my lips. "I want you to suck my cock like a good little girl," he murmurs against my lips.

My stomach flips, and I hate the eagerness I feel as I drop to my knees in front of him.

Dante smirks at me as if he's won. Maybe he has. I'm too

overtaken with lust to care right now as I press my hand against his muscular abdomen, slowly dragging the waistband of his boxer briefs down.

His huge, thick cock bobs up in front of my face, dripping with a stream of pearly precum. He's by far the biggest I've ever set eyes on, let alone taken into my mouth—just looking at his cock makes my jaw ache. It also makes my mouth water. The thought of tasting the man I've longed for so intimately. I let my tongue gently lap up the precum dripping from the tip, feeling the desire tighten inside of me.

Slowly, I open my mouth and slip the head of his hard, throbbing cock into my mouth. The taste of him is pure masculinity, as I run the tip of my tongue gently around the tip of him.

Dante groans, shutting his eyes as I take more of him into my throat. I struggle not to gag as he slips further than I'd intended. His fist tightens in my hair as he takes control. More of his cum spills down my throat, increasing the need inside of me.

I've never felt so eager to get a man off in all my life. It's odd considering I hated him not long ago. Dante makes me feel so twisted up inside.

I start to suck him deeper into my throat, breathing through my nose. My saliva spills all over his cock, dripping onto his balls. Dante growls like a beast as he takes total control of the situation. He thrusts his cock deep into my throat with such force it feels like I'm going to choke. I try to breathe through my nose, but it's impossible.

I dig my nails into his thighs as I try to push him away to

get air. He doesn't let up, continuing to take my throat with all his strength. Finally, I manage to push him away. "Fuck, I can't breathe," I gasp.

Dante grabs my throat hard, angling my eyes up to meet his. "Good. I own you now, Violet, and I decide if you can or can't breathe."

I swallow hard, scared by the look in his eyes. The darkness in them is all-consuming, and it has no limits.

"Open up, princess."

I open my mouth, watching as his cock moves closer to my mouth. Initially, he rests the head of his cock on my tongue, leaking cum all over it. There's a flood of need that consumes me as he drives his cock deep into the back of my throat. I try not to gag, but he's too forceful.

Slowly, I manage to get into a rhythm despite my jaw aching like hell. I am drooling all over his huge cock, struggling to take each thrust he gives.

He stops and grabs my hair forcefully, making me look up at him as he spits into my mouth. "You're my dirty little princess, aren't you?" he growls.

I'm too gone to deny it. "Yes, daddy." I open my mouth, eager for him to give me his cock again.

"I hope you're hungry for my cum, baby girl. I'm going to cum down your pretty little throat."

Before I can reply, he takes my throat again, thrusting relentlessly as he uses me so damn good. It shocks me how much I love being dominated by him, something I'd never even thought about. He grunts above me as his cock twitches against the back of my throat, warning me he's close.

"Swallow daddy's come like a good girl," he growls as he releases rope after rope of thick, salty cum down my throat. I swallow, but it's almost impossible to keep up, and some of it spills out of my mouth.

I swallow most of it, wipe whatever spilled out of my mouth with my finger and lick it off seductively. Dante's eyes are full of desire, but there's something else in his expression—something that looks a lot like regret. It makes my stomach twist with nerves.

He lies down on his back, resting his hands behind his head and shutting his eyes. "Lie down against me," he orders.

I do as he says, realizing that he doesn't intend to get me off in return. I have too much pride to be so needy as to beg him to do it or take care of myself with him in the bed. Utterly spent, I rest my head against his warm chest and fall asleep, feeling the throb of need between my thighs.

I WAKE THE NEXT MORNING, opening my eyes to see Dante's tattooed chest rising and falling as he sleeps by my side. It irritates me that a throb ignites between my thighs, and my pussy gets wet at the sight of him half-naked. It doesn't help that last night I sucked him off, and it was hot as hell, but he left me needy and unsatisfied. Dante didn't touch me where I so badly needed him to touch me.

What the fuck have I agreed to?

Last night I signed what little freedom I still had away to the monster lying by my side. I lift a hand to my head as it is pounding. The wine last night kept flowing, and I kept drinking.

My heart skips a beat as I remember the line I crossed. Dante is ruthless. He fucked my throat so hard I thought he was going to choke me with his huge length.

The darkness that lies within Dante is beyond anything I can fathom. He's sick, twisted, and doesn't mind taking what he wants. The sickest part about it is that I'm intrigued by that part of him and attracted to his dominance.

It makes little sense considering my past experiences, but I think it has something to do with Dante being the literal polar opposite of my stepdad. He was weak and pathetic, drunk all the damn time. Dante is powerful, unapologetic, and that is something that lures me in like a fish to the bait.

I turn over onto my back and stare at the ceiling, wondering if this is happening to me. A few days ago, if you'd told me I'd wake up sleeping next to Dante Ortega, I would have been happier than anything. I'm torn between wanting to be happy that we finally crossed the line between flirting and doing something about our attraction and hating the man lying next to me.

He stirs suddenly and turns over, wrapping an arm around my waist. "Buenos días, princess," he purrs into my ear.

I tense at his touch, hating the way electricity pulses through my veins.

He growls softly. "Remember, you are my fiancé now. Act like it."

I swallow hard. "Does this mean I won't have to stay locked in this room anymore?" I glance over at him.

His dark brown eyes are filled with such fiery, passionate desire I feel the slickness pooling between my thighs. The memory of his thick, long cock pounding in and out of my mouth returns, and I'm so turned on.

"No, you can roam the house and gardens. However, Pedro will be with you at all times. He's going to be your bodyguard."

"Bodyguard?" I ask.

Dante nods. "Yes, I have many enemies, and I won't risk your safety." He pauses, looking into my eyes. "Not to mention, I have to make sure you don't try to run."

Bastard.

"So, you've got me a babysitter?" I ask, freeing myself from his grasp and swinging my legs out of bed.

Dante stands from the bed and heads toward the door that adjoins his room. "You should be happy I'm allowing you out of this room at all." He glances back at me with a cold, hard stare. "Enjoy it while it lasts." He opens the door and disappears without another word.

I clench my fists around the duvet, feeling angrier than I've felt in a long time. Dante is an asshole. I'm angry at him. I'm angrier at myself for agreeing to his stupid fucking agreement. I could try to convince myself that Dante didn't give me a choice, but that's a lie. The contract made my obligations clear, and I still signed it of my own will.

The one thing I can't understand is why he'd want me to consider becoming his wife. Dante strikes me as the kind of guy that likes to take any woman he wants. He doesn't strike me as the kind of guy ready to settle down with a wife and children.

The dread I felt the moment I'd signed the contract last night returns. I've signed my soul to the devil, and the worst thing about it is I don't know what he truly wants from me. I guess only time will tell.

1 2

DANTE

I walk into the board room and Javier is already there, sitting at the right side of my chair. He's always early, which is why I'm early. I need him to tell my father that I won't marry Rosa Duarte, who he picked out for me.

It's been three days since I got Violet to sign the contract—three days since I shoved my cock down her throat and made her choke on it. I haven't visited her since, and it's driving me insane.

"Javier, just the man I wanted to speak to."

Javier looks up from his notebook with wide eyes. "Dante, I didn't expect you to be here early."

I shrug. "We need to talk. Have you got a moment?"

He bows his head and puts away his notebook. "Always, sir."

I clap him on the shoulder as I take my seat. "Good. I need you to send a message to my father."

Javier swallows hard and pales. I know he hates being the go-between. My father is a ruthless man, but Javier has always known how to handle him. "I see. What message?"

"Tell him that I'm engaged to be married to an American girl."

Javier's brow furrows. "You want me to lie to your father?"

Lying to my father would be a death sentence, and Javier knows I wouldn't risk his life like that. "No, it's not a lie. Violet has agreed to trial run an engagement with me."

Javier looks at me like I've lost my mind. "Violet. Are you sure that's a good idea?"

I grit my teeth as I hate being questioned, even by my best friend. "I hope you aren't questioning my decisions, Javier."

He shakes his head. "Never, jefe, but I'm here to make sure you make the right decisions. Does Violet want to marry you?"

I shake my head. "It's not set-in stone yet. She's signed a contract that she will give me two months to prove I can make her happy as my fiancé."

Javier sighs heavily. "And, if you can't?"

I glare at my second in command. This guy is seriously questioning what will happen if I can't make a woman happy. Violet is already hooked on me, even if she wouldn't admit it. "I will."

Javier knows when to stop pushing me, so he nods. "Alright, I'll get the word out to him. He won't be very happy, though, and neither will Gerardo Duarte."

"Do I look like I give a fuck what Gerardo Duarte thinks?"

Javier shakes his head, smiling. "Nope, you don't."

"What time is the contractor supposed to be here?"

Javier glances at his watch. "Three minutes ago."

I grit my teeth. "They aren't making a very good impression. Maybe we should try and find a more reliable company."

"No, boss. You know this company is the best. They're probably held up in traffic."

I narrow my eyes at Javier, drumming my fingers on the table impatiently. It bugs me that ever since I've kidnapped Violet, she's all I can think about day and night. It's the reason I've forced myself to stay away from her these past three days, to test my resolve. This contract for the new bar is important and yet I feel bored by the formalities.

"Ring them and find out how long they will be."

Javier pulls out his phone without a word and dials a number. I hate being made to wait at the best of times.

"Hey, where are you guys?" Javier's brow furrows, and his eyes widen. "Fuck, okay, we'll rearrange."

"What is it?" I ask as he puts the phone down.

He shakes his head. "Someone is fucking with us. The team coming to meet us were rammed off the road in a hit and run."

I slam my hand down on the table. "It's the fucking Irish, again."

Javier shrugs. "We don't know for sure, but a mole must be feeding information from inside the cartel. It doesn't make sense how they'd know about the meeting." He shakes his head. "Luckily, they're just a little roughed up, not dead."

Great.

Another fucking problem to deal with.

I point at Javier. "I want you to go down to the contractors for a meeting with whoever is in charge and get this deal signed and sealed. After that, find out who the rat is in our outfit and bring the bastard to me."

Javier nods. "On it, jefe." He stands and heads out of our office's boardroom, leaving me reeling over this most recent attack. The Irish don't want us to further our operations here because our drugs are better than the shit they pedal. We've overtaken them in recent years in terms of power in the city, and we've even had quite a few distributors move from buying Irish supplied drugs to ours, which are by far superior.

Devlin Murphy knows how to hold a grudge, and I would bet anything on his gang being behind the hit and run on the contractors. They want to stop our expansion in any way possible. I tried to send him a message a few months back, sending one of my men to kill him. It backfired spectacularly when my man got killed, and since then, he's been more ruthless than ever.

Ric walks past the window of the boardroom and pokes his head in. "Where are the contractors?"

I shake my head. "Don't ask."

Ric raises a brow. "Bad day?"

"You can say that again." I stand from my chair and walk toward the door.

"Want to grab a drink?" Ric asks.

I glance at my watch, noticing it's only eleven o'clock in the morning. "Bit early, isn't it?"

He laughs. "Is it ever too early? We can get something to eat too if that will make you feel better. I'm starving."

"Fair enough. Let's go down to El Torrero. I need to catch Carlos off guard and get the money he owes me. Javier gave him a week to pay, and it's up."

Ric raises a brow. "Surprised you would want to go there now your girlfriend doesn't work there anymore."

I growl. Ric always knows how to push my buttons. "Do you want me to knock you out? I need to get the money Carlos owes me and tell him we're not playing the Friday night spot anymore."

The knowing smirk that curves onto Ric's lips pisses me off. He knows why I don't want to play there anymore. My only reason for keeping the spot is now locked away in my home. He doesn't point that out, though. He knows when to keep his mouth shut.

CARLOS IS BEHIND THE BAR, shouting at one of his bartenders as she stares down at the floor. He sounds pissed. I'm about to make his day a whole lot worse.

"Carlos."

He tenses at the sound of my voice, slowly turning around to face me. "Mi Amigo. How are you?"

I narrow my eyes at him. "I'd be a lot better if I didn't have to chase you around the city."

Carlos pales. "I wasn't aware you were trying to get a hold of me."

"Cut the bullshit. I've tried to ring you enough times." I clap my hands. "Have a seat."

Carlos walks out from behind the bar and sits at the table I'd chosen. He may be the boss of this place, but he knows who runs Queens. Ric has his meanest glare on as he sits opposite the man who has been trying to give me the runaround.

I'm the last to sit, leaning back in the chair casually. "You owe me a lot of money, Carlos." Two-hundred thousand dollars, to be exact. Since he took a huge portion of my last shipment of cocaine and hasn't paid for it, my father won't be too happy if the money isn't deposited soon.

Carlos swallows, nodding his head. "I know. I need a little more time."

I glance at Ric and laugh. "Do you hear that, Ric? He wants more time."

Ric starts to laugh, too, making Carlos even more uncomfortable than he already was. The power rush I feel making men like Carlos quake is exhilarating. I haven't gone after a debt repayment myself for a long while, and I miss the rush. We both fall silent and glare at the man opposite.

Ric leans forward. "Are you fucking insane? The Ortega Cartel doesn't give people more time to pay for the product. Javier gave you an extra week and you were lucky he didn't ask me first."

Carlos looks at me. "We're friends. I thought you might give me——"

I hold my hand up, cutting him off. "Friend or not, this is business. Do you think Raúl Ortega is happy to sit and wait for his money because his son is friends with the guy that we sold his coke to?"

The mention of my father ignites a fear so intense in Carlos's eyes I'm pretty sure he's about to pee his pants. He shakes his head. "No. I've got most of it in the back."

"Most of it isn't good enough. I need every fucking penny you owe me by midnight tonight."

Carlos will come through. He may not have the cash right now, but I know he has the means to get it. "Alright. I'll have it for you." He glances back at the bar. "Do you want me to get you what I've got now?"

I shake my head. "No, you come by my house before midnight tonight and drop it all off. I don't have to tell you what happens if you don't"

Carlos shakes his head. "No, you don't." A few moments of tense silence pass between us. "I have to ask you something." I tense, knowing that he's about to bring up Violet going missing on Friday night. "Did something happen with Violet on Friday?" His brow furrows. "No one has seen her since she went out back to take the trash out, and…"

I nod. "Violet won't be working for you anymore, Carlos. We won't be playing here on Friday nights anymore either."

"Ya vali madre," he swears, running a hand across his bald head. "I seriously rely on you guys to pull in a lot of customers on Friday nights."

I shrug. "It's not our problem. It's not like you rely on the profits from this shit hole to live anyway."

"Fair enough." He looks irritated, but he wouldn't have the balls to fight me on this. If he did, he would lose more than a gig on a Friday night. "Do you guys want a drink or something to eat?"

Ric nods. "Fuck yeah, I'm starving. Get me my usual."

"I'll have the same," I say.

Carlos nods. "Sure thing, I'll get Enrique to cook your food fresh, and Alice will bring your drinks over in a moment." He stands and glances at me one more time. "I'll be over tonight with the cash."

I don't respond, watching him as he walks away from us.

"Can you believe the nerve on that guy, asking for more time?" Ric says, voice full of disbelief.

I don't take my eyes off him until he has disappeared to the back of the bar. "Maybe we've gone too soft lately, Ric. What do you think?"

He laughs. "You've always been too soft."

"Fuck you," I say, punching him in the shoulder. "I'm being serious. Do you think we need to start sending a message to the runners on the street?" If Carlos thinks he can be a few weeks late on a payment for drugs he had six weeks ago, he doesn't respect us. "Carlos had the balls to pay late. If word gets out that we've not held people accountable, we could end up with more problems on our hands."

Ric nods. "True. Are you saying you want to make an example out of Carlos?"

Since I moved from Mexico to New York City, Carlos has been a friend. Even so, I can't rule out making an example of him if he crosses the line again. I shake my head. "Only if he doesn't come through with the cash by midnight."

"Anyone else fucks with us after this, we will come down hard," he says, as Alice approaches us with our drinks.

"Hey guys, I've got your double rums." She sets Ric's down first in front of him and then mine.

"Thanks," Ric says, winking at her.

She flushes and shoots him a shy smile before rushing back behind the bar.

This place feels soulless without my firecracker standing behind it. It brings back so many memories of her watching me with a desire that set my soul ablaze. Now, she looks at me with a hatred that somehow has the same effect. I can't wait to get back to her. I can't wait to make her mine for real.

Once she has had a taste, I know that she'll never go back. The biggest complication is the feelings that are starting to rear their ugly head. I know getting involved with Vi is dangerous because of our history. She has an effect on me like no other woman ever has. It's deep and profound, and I know how dangerous that is in the world I operate in.

VIOLET

*I*t's my third day of freedom since I signed the contract Dante presented me with. Since that night he fell asleep in my room, he has left me alone. It only makes the anticipation grow as I know he wants more than a blow job from me—it was clear in the contract I signed.

Initially, it wasn't clear how much freedom I have to explore the grounds. Pedro, the bodyguard Dante assigned to me, has slowly started to warm to me and I to him. He told me he'd happily take me out into the grounds today.

I'm not allowed to go anywhere without him in case I try and escape. I can't deny that it is nice to get some fresh air. That house was driving me crazy.

Dante may not have visited me again, but I'm not sure what this small amount of freedom will cost me in the long term. I sigh heavily, trying not to think about that right now.

"How large are the grounds of this place?" I call back to

Pedro, who purposely keeps behind me even though I've asked him to walk with me numerous times.

He mutters something under his breath in Spanish. "Three acres. I said I'd take you into the grounds, but I'm not your damn tour guide, señorita."

I smile. "Sorry, but you are the only person who can answer my questions, so you are going to have to get used to it." I glance back at him, smiling.

He rolls his eyes, but there's a whisper of a smile there too. Slowly, I'm starting to melt away his cold exterior, and I know we're going to get on. We walk in easy silence, and Pedro closes the gap between us, walking by my side.

"Any tips on where to explore first?" I ask, glancing at him.

He sighs, resigned to the fact he's stuck with me. "Yeah, the lake is a pretty nice place for a walk. I'll take you down there."

"Sounds good." We walk with only the sounds of birds tweeting. "How long have you worked for Mr. Ortega?" I ask.

He raises a brow as if he's surprised that I'm asking him a question. "Not long. About a year."

"Do you like working for him?"

He looks a little reluctant about answering that question. "Why?"

"I just wonder what kind of employer he is."

Pedro continues to walk at a slightly faster pace looking a little tense. "He's a fair employer." He doesn't elaborate and changes the subject. "How did you wind up here?" His eyes linger at the faint bruise on my neck, making my cheeks heat.

I look down at the floor, feeling a sadness tug at my chest. "Saw something I shouldn't have seen."

Pedro nods. "That's tough. I'm surprised you're still alive, though."

I look up at him, and the expression on his face is curious. He wants to ask me more but clears his throat instead. "There's the lake," he says, nodding ahead of himself to a sparkling body of water in the distance.

There are old willow trees spread out around the edge with their long, dangling curtain-like branches and leaves stretching toward the surface. A swan and some ducks swim on top of the water as birds sing in the trees. It's surprisingly peaceful since we're still in New York, most likely thanks to the dense woodland behind the lake. "It's beautiful."

"It's my favorite place on the estate. I come up here on nice days for my lunch break." He smiles easily at me. Considering Pedro is employed by Dante's criminal empire, he seems like a decent guy.

He leads me to the water's edge and sheepishly digs into his pocket, pulling out an old piece of bread. "I stole it from the kitchen in case the chance arose." He holds it out to me. "Do you want to feed the ducks?"

I smile as this day is turning out far better than I expected. Pedro and I are well on our way to becoming friends. "I'd like that." I take the piece of bread and start to tear pieces off throwing them to the ducks, feeling childish but happy.

Even my childhood never felt like this. All my life, it feels like I've been followed by loss and heartbreak. When I was three years old, my dad died fighting for the military. At least I always had my mom, and we were inseparable through my early years of life until I was about ten years old, and she remarried to a man called Hank. I wasn't keen on him, and he was always horrible to me. Worse when my mom got sick, and he started to demand things that no stepdad should ever ask for.

My life took a turn darker than I ever expected when my mom lost her two-year battle with cancer six years ago. She left me with my stepdad, who couldn't cope with my mother's death without drinking even more than he did when she was sick. His abuse took a turn for the worse, so I saved as much money as possible and moved up to New York from Florida.

The sun beats down on my skin and warms me right to my core. I love the sound of the bird singing in the trees. It's so peaceful here, and for a moment, I forget all my worries about Dante.

It's a freeing experience being out in the fresh air. I may have only been locked in that room for two days and stuck in the house for five, but it felt longer. Quickly, I missed the fresh air and the feel of the wind against my face.

The ducks begin to swim silently over to me, noticing that there's food. They quack happily, grabbing the small bits of bread I throw. Even amidst all this beauty and peacefulness, I can't seem to get Dante off my mind.

The contract I signed was a trial run engagement with strings attached. I can't understand why Dante would want to marry me since he has shown no sign of tenderness.

He fucked my throat, fell asleep, and then walked away with hardly a look in my direction. It stung because a sick and twisted part of me wondered if perhaps he had feelings for me all along. He may be a criminal, but I thought our connection could have been real.

Three days I've waited, wondering when he will demand more. Each night I hear him in the room next to mine, pacing the floor before going to bed. I want answers to so many questions, but I know he wouldn't give them to me even if I asked.

The wind picks up, and I tighten my cardigan around myself, throwing the last piece of bread into the water.

Pedro is on guard, surveying the area. I can't understand what threat there would be to anyone on Dante's property.

"Shall we continue?" I ask.

He smiles. "Sure, let's walk around the lake." He leads the way along a pretty gravel path lined with wildflowers.

I almost walk right into his back as he comes to a sudden halt.

"Did you hear that?"

My brow furrows. "What?"

"The snap of a branch underfoot." He turns around and stares into the woodland. "Someone is in the woods."

"Could it be one of the guards?" I ask since I've seen half a dozen of them at least patrolling the house and gardens today alone.

Pedro shakes his head. "They don't patrol the woodland." He grabs my wrist and pushes me behind him. "Stay behind me."

I gasp as he pulls a gun out of his pocket—every muscle in my body trembles as a rush of adrenaline courses through my veins. A branch snaps ahead of us in the woodland, followed by a gunshot that misses the two of us by barely in an inch.

"Fuck," Pedro exclaims, aiming his gun toward the woods and shooting twice. "I can't fucking see them."

I cling onto his jacket, feeling utterly useless. "Shouldn't we run?"

Pedro shakes his head. "If we run, we're an open target with our backs turned. Trust me."

It's strange that I do trust him, even though I don't know him. There's another shot, and Pedro cries out in agony. He's been hit, and there's blood splattered all over my clothes from his wound. The danger we're both in scares me.

I try to help him stay standing, but he's growing heavy against me. "Pedro, we need to get out of here."

He shakes his head. "Move back slowly toward the cover of the trees behind us."

I glance behind us and see a few sparse trees at the edge of the lake. Slowly, I walk back, holding him up. Pedro is focusing on the woodlands as we make it to the trees.

He manages to stay standing until we make it behind the tree trunk, offering us a small amount of cover. Pedro has been shot in the shoulder and lower abdomen. I press my hand against the wound at his abdomen. "We need to stop the bleeding."

He shakes his head, reaching for the radio on his belt. "We need backup."

I continue to put pressure on his wounds, keeping them hidden behind the trunk of the tree. A shot hits the tree, making my heart accelerate.

Pedro speaks in Spanish, calling for help. He drops the radio to the ground, looking exhausted. I notice his gun to one side and pick it up. "How are we going to survive this?"

He meets my gaze. "Whatever happens, you get yourself out of here if you get the chance. Leave me here."

I shake my head. "No chance. You saved my life."

"It's my job," he says, wincing as blood gushes from his shoulder. I rip off my cardigan and struggle to tear it in half and bunch up the fabric. I grab Pedro's hand and force it against the fabric, pressing it to his shoulder.

"Hold that over the wound while I cover the other one."

He glares at me. "They are getting closer, listen," he whispers.

I stop still, keeping my hand pressed against the fabric. The faint thud of footsteps carries on the wind toward us.

I swallow hard.

Suddenly, I hear someone shout from the other side of the tree, dangerously close. The backup Pedro called has arrived. I watch in shock as they open fire on the attackers with machine guns. I keep my hand pressed on Pedro's wound and keep my eyes on it too.

It's almost impossible to think this is my life now—a life filled with danger, guns, and criminals. Almost a week ago, I was a bartender with a crush on a man I thought was a normal musician.

I think it's clear that I underestimated how dangerous Dante is. I knew he was a criminal, but this attack on his grounds tells me his criminal activity involvement is far more serious than anything I could have imagined. Not to mention, the artillery his guards are packing is beyond any standard security crew.

A man comes over to me and grabs me by the waist, lifting me over his shoulder.

Is this what my life has become now?

The life of a timid, helpless damsel that needs rescuing from every situation. It irritates me more than I can put into words, especially after all the shit I've been through to get to this point in life. I don't need rescuing and never have, yet a week in Dante's capture has reduced me to someone I no longer recognize.

14

DANTE

I barge through the front door as panic grips around my heart. Violet has been attacked on my fucking property. Whoever is responsible will have to answer to me. Violet is innocent in all of this, and no one is aware of our arrangement—not yet anyway.

"Where is she, Angela?" I ask.

"Resting in her room, sir." I rush up the stairs before she can finish her sentence. "The doctor is with her, and she is fine."

Fine. That word angers me more than I can put into words. Violet isn't fine. The first fucking day, I let her out of this house, and she's been attacked on my grounds. Pedro managed to save her, but now he's had to be admitted to our on-site hospital.

None of this is fine. I rush through the corridor and charge into Violet's room.

Her eyes open at my intrusion, and she meets my gaze. Instantly she relaxes when she sees that it's me. Tears fill her eyes, but she doesn't let them fall. I rush over to her without a word and sit down on the bed. "I'm so sorry I wasn't here." I clench my jaw, knowing that showing her too much care is a mistake.

She shakes her head. "Is Pedro okay?"

"Fuck Pedro," I growl. "Are you okay?"

Her brow furrows, and she sits up straighter. "I'm okay because Pedro saved my life."

I shake my head and turn my attention to Jose, the resident doctor, as I couldn't care less about one of the bodyguards in my outfit. "How is she?"

He nods. "She is in a bit of shock, but other than that, she's unharmed."

My increased heart rate starts to steady the moment the doctor says she's unharmed. I grit my teeth, wishing the panic I'd felt hadn't been there. My feelings for Violet have always been too deep.

Jose packs his bag. "I'll be off now, sir, if that is all."

I nod in response. "Yes, thank you, Jose."

Violet clears her throat. "Have you seen Pedro at all?" she asks the doctor.

Jose shakes his head. "No, I'm heading back to the on-site hospital. I'll be checking in on his situation."

She sighs heavily, looking concerned. What is it about Pedro that has her so concerned? I can't help but feel a twinge of jealousy that she can't stop asking about him.

Jose walks out of the room, leaving us alone.

I return my attention to Violet, searching her crystal blue eyes. "What happened?"

Violet draws in a deep breath. "I honestly don't know. It all happened so fast."

I take her hand in mine. "Where were you when they attacked?"

She bites the inside of her cheek as if worried about telling me where she was. "Pedro took me down to the lake, and we were half-way around it when the first shot was fired."

I feel my blood starting to boil at the thought of Violet being under fire like that. "Did you get a look at the attacker?"

She shakes her head. "They hid in the woods." Tears flood her eyes. "Pedro blocked me with his body and tried to shoot them, but he took two bullets before the other guards arrived and scared the attackers off." Violet pulls her hand from mine. "What kind of crazy shit are you involved in any way?" She looks me in the eye. "Who are you?"

A question I'm surprised she didn't ask sooner. Maybe she was too scared of learning the answer. "I'm Dante Ortega, boss of the Ortega Cartel operations in New York City." I watch her reaction to my answer. "My father is the head of the family operations down in Mexico."

Her throat bobs softly as she swallows. "Fuck," she mutters.

The sound of that word on her lips drives me wild. "Exactly what I was thinking," I say, grabbing her throat. "I want to fuck you, princess."

Her eyes widen, and her nostrils flare. "No," She says, shaking her head.

I tilt my head to the side, noticing her eyes are dilated with desire. "Are you forgetting the agreement you signed?"

A flash of cold hatred enters her eyes as she stares at me with a rage that makes my blood boil. "No." Her response is cold and fast.

The need to be inside of her is strong. I grit my teeth, trying to fight the desire to ravage her. "I need to be inside of you, Vi," I mutter, stroking my hand down her soft, creamy chest.

Her breasts heave as she breathes in sharply. I bring my lips to her collarbone and nibble the skin softly. Every muscle in her body is tense.

"Dante, I don't want—"

I cover her lips with mine, silencing her before she can tell me this isn't what she wants. Violet is tense against me for a moment before relaxing and allowing me to kiss her. My tongue searches every inch of her mouth as desperation to claim her consumes me.

I bite her bottom lip, wanting to taste and own every inch of her body—inside and out. My cock throbs in the confines of my tight boxer briefs. Desperate to break free and bury itself as deep as fucking possible inside Violet's perfect, tight pussy.

I suck on her tongue, making her moan. It's a sweet, raspy sound that drives me wild. There isn't anything that could stop me from taking her now. She will be bound, red and panting beneath me all night long.

"Strip," I order, retreating from her and heading toward the door to my room. "I'll be back in a moment." I don't glance back to see if she is following my order because I know she will.

Violet is about to learn my twisted tastes. My bedroom preferences are difficult for most women to accept, but since Violet signed that contract, she doesn't get a choice for two months.

I enter my closet and grab my blindfold, collar, ropes, flogger, and a ball gag. Violet might think I'm a monster, but she hasn't seen anything yet. When I return to the room, she is lying naked on the top of the duvet.

I pause a moment and take in the vision in front of me. Violet's eyes are shut, and her golden blonde hair is falling in waves all over the pillow elegantly. I groan at the sight of her firm breasts with hard nipples exposed and the way she has her legs open.

"You're so beautiful, princess."

Her eyes snap open and meet mine. The passion in them is intense, and I can't tell if it's hatred or lust burning in those crystal blue eyes. They move from my eyes to the instruments in my hands. "What is all that for?"

I don't reply as it's obvious. Instead, I approach the bed, setting some of the equipment down. "Kneel in front of me."

Violet stares at me blankly.

"Don't make me repeat myself, Vi."

The column of her throat bobs as she swallows hard. "And, if I refuse?"

"I wouldn't if I were you. Kneel," I order.

She narrows her eyes and moves onto her knees in front of me, glaring at me with anger.

I grab the silk blindfold and walk around the bed so that I'm standing behind her. She draws in a deep breath as I place the blindfold over her eyes and fasten it. I notice her shiver as I gently brush my hands over her shoulders.

I grab her two wrists in front of her and tie the rope around them, so she is restricted. I normally like to be a bit more adventurous with my bindings, but I know taking this too far too quickly will lose any chance of Violet getting hooked on me and the lifestyle I crave.

Violet sucks in a deep breath. "Dante, I'm not sure about this."

"Stop overthinking things." I return to stand in front of her and press my lips to hers and kiss her deeply. "Trust me, baby girl. Daddy's going to make you feel so good you will think you've died and gone to heaven."

Her body tenses. "How can I trust you?"

"Take a leap of faith and let me show you what you've been missing."

She shudders as I pick up the collar. I want to put it on her as a symbol to mark that she belongs to me. Carefully, I unbuckle the leather collar and place it around her dainty neck and do it up.

"W-what are you going to do to me?"

I drag my teeth softly across her shoulder. "Fuck you like you've never been fucked before."

Violet whimpers, and it's the most satisfying sound.

I glance at the ball gag, wondering if it is a step too far for our first session. I've taken away her sight, so that will do for now. I toss the gag onto the nightstand and focus all my attention on the beauty kneeling before me. I roughly grab her bound wrists and drag her around, pushing her face down into the bed.

She shivers in anticipation, but I'm certain she has no idea what will come next. My fingers wrap around the leather handle of the flogger, and I gently brush it across the creamy, smooth skin of her ass.

"You've been a bad girl, Violet, making me wait to have you," I say, moving the flogger across her skin slowly. "Do you know what happens to bad girls?"

She's silent, clearly not aware that I'm expecting an answer.

"Answer me," I growl.

"No, I've got no idea, Dante. Please don't—"

I bring the flogger up and strike it against her tender flesh, making her yelp in pain. Instantly her pale skin turns bright pink from the force. "I told you to call me daddy."

She whimpers again, louder this time. "Sorry, daddy," she breathes.

I run a finger through her soaking wet pussy, groaning at the juice dripping from her onto the bedsheets. She's so turned on. I gently brush my finger over her clit.

"Fuck," she moans, her thighs quivering.

I bring the flogger down on her ass again, making her cry out in pain. "Do you like being punished, baby girl?"

There are a moments of silence as she pants heavily. "Yes, daddy," she moans, unable to hide the need in her voice.

I lean down and kiss the sensitive flesh of her ass where I struck her. Violet has been on my mind for two years, and finally, I have her where I've dreamed she'd be—at my mercy being totally and utterly dominated.

After flogging her ass a couple more times so that it's stinging red, I bury my face between her thighs. Her back arches as I press my tongue deep inside of her, tasting her for the first time. The sweet taste of honey isn't as sweet as her.

Violet shudders as I keep her legs wide open for me. I reach forward and rub her clit, making her moan. Her thighs tremble violently as she comes apart, juice gushing from her pussy. My mouth waters as I lap up every drop, consuming her entirely.

I will possess Violet in every way before the night is through. After that, no one will dare try and take her from me again, or I'll make sure they die a slow and painful death.

15

VIOLET

*D*ante is a beast, and I'm his prey.

The pleasure courses through my body from my last orgasm as he ruthlessly pushes me higher and higher with each thrust of his finger or lick of his tongue again.

It's unbelievable how much being blindfolded increases every sensation. The pain he inflicted only adds to the excruciating pleasure that he gives me. I've never wanted to come as bad as I do right now.

I wanted so badly to refuse his advances. The moment his lips were on mine, I couldn't help it. My reasoning flew out of the window, and all I could think about was his touch. We've both longed for this moment for so long.

My ass stings, but it makes the pleasure more intense. Dante digs his fingertips hard into my hips and continues to devour me, pushing me closer and closer to release, only to back off when I'm on the edge of the cliff.

"Please, daddy," I moan, arching my back as he yet again dangles me on the edge. "I need to come," I beg, shocking myself that he has reduced me to a begging, needy excuse of a woman.

Dante growls like an animal, yanking my hair hard. "Tell me why you deserve to come again, princess."

I swallow hard. "Because I've been a good girl."

He groans. "Have you now?"

I don't answer, knowing it's rhetorical.

He lets go of my hair, pushing me back down against the bed hard. "You don't get to come until my cock is buried as deep inside of you as physically possible."

I tense at the thought of his huge cock stretching me more than I've ever been stretched.

"Relax, princess," he murmurs into my ear. "Daddy's going to fuck you like you've always dreamed of."

I swallow hard, knowing that he's right. His roughness is addictive, and I know that now I have had a taste I won't be able to stop. His cock teases through my entrance, coating the tip in my juices. Anticipation swells inside of me. My loss of sight makes every touch and sound more intense.

Suddenly, he grabs my bound wrists forcefully and pushes my back down on the bed. The blindfold blocks out everything as I try to get a sense of where he is. I feel the weight of his cock resting against my clit as he looms over me.

I hold my breath, anticipating the invasion of his huge length. It feels like hours slip by as I wait, listening to his heavy breathing above me.

"Tell me how badly you want my cock, princess."

His order only increases the need inside of me. Dante is teasing me without mercy, making me wait to come.

"I want it so badly, daddy," I say, wishing I could pull him inside. "Please give me your cock."

He groans, rubbing his cock through my soaking wet lips. Each time he bumps my clit, I feel myself getting closer and closer to climax. If he doesn't hurry up, I will come again before he's inside me.

"Dante," I moan his name, trying to warn him.

He stops as I'm on the edge of release. I'm so desperate to come I almost feel like crying.

"Don't stop," I complain.

He kisses me softly, and the need tightens my stomach. "Haven't you heard that delayed gratification is the best kind?" he purrs into my ear, before biting my earlobe.

Fuck.

He is toying with me. That's what I am—his toy to do with as he wants. I bite my bottom lip between my teeth, trying desperately to stop myself from begging him shamelessly for his cock.

He starts over and over again, bringing me close to the edge, only to take it away at the last moment. In the end, it's too much.

"Please, Dante," I cry, writhing in the sheets. "I need to come," I pant, feeling unshed tears prickling at my eyes. It's almost painful how badly I need to come.

He stills and wraps his large hand around my throat, squeezing hard enough to cut off my supply of oxygen. "Daddy is in control here, princess. When you finally come with my cock buried inside of you, it will be the best damn orgasm you've ever had." He licks a path up the column of my neck, making me shudder. "I'm going to be the best lover you've ever had and the last one you'll ever have too." He bites my collarbone hard. "You are mine, Violet."

I shudder, resigned to the fact that I have no control. My body turns limp beneath Dante as he continues to drive me toward the edge again. This time, as I'm getting close, he slides every inch of his thick cock deep inside of me with one thrust.

"Fuck," I cry, as the walls of my pussy clutch onto him, dragging him deeper. My whole body convulses at the intensity of my orgasm. For a moment, it's like my brain stops functioning, and there's nothing but blank white flooding my mind. The hot, white pleasure takes control of every atom of my being.

"That's it, princess, come on daddy's cock like a good girl."

His dirty talk only makes the pleasure spike higher than I thought physically possible. Before Dante's even started to fuck me, he's already by far the best lover I've ever had. No man has ever made me come at all.

He starts to fuck me slowly, building that need inside me before my last orgasm has even passed. I've never felt such intense pleasure in my twenty-four years—nothing has come close.

Dante grunts above me like a wild animal, fucking me harder with every thrust of his cock. Before the aftershock of the most intense orgasm wears off, I feel myself coming undone again.

"Oh fuck," I cry, wishing I could dig my fingers through

Dante's short hair or touch his hard muscles. "Fuck me harder, daddy," I beg, utterly lost to the way he's making me feel.

"That's it, princess. I want to feel you come on my cock over and over again until you're so tired you can hardly stay awake," Dante growls, grabbing my hips forcefully and flipping me onto my front. He takes a fistful of my hair and yanks it, forcing me to arch my back.

The pain radiating through my scalp only makes the pleasure better—better than I ever could have dreamed. He pounds into me harder, one hand tangled in my hair and the other around my throat so that I can't breathe so freely. For a moment, it feels like I lift up out of my body. As if I'm no longer alive and the intense, white-hot pleasure is my new state of being.

Dante let's go of my throat, and I feel a head rush as he continues to fuck me like a beast. He spanks my ass hard, bringing me back to the present. It's all too much as the pleasure crashes into me again and I come undone. Exhaustion like I've never felt consumes me, but Dante continues to fuck me through my fourth or fifth orgasm. I'm so muddled I can't even remember how many times I've come. Each orgasm seems to blend into the next, consuming me entirely.

I feel tears fall from my eyes as I try to keep up with him. It's impossible. I'm entirely spent as I remain limp in his grasp, fucked like a doll. That's all I am to him a toy to be bent to his will as he sees fit.

My fantasies of Dante over the past two years never included me being bound and blindfolded. It's something I didn't think I'd enjoy, but it's the most amazing experience I've ever had. He has me at his mercy, and all I can do is submit. His dominance is like a drug that I don't think I'll ever get enough of.

"Dante, I can't take it anymore," I manage to rasp out, hoping that he'll go easy on me.

He bites my shoulder softly, grunting as he continues to fuck me. "You will take my cock like a good girl, princess. Daddy wants to feel you come one more time."

I shudder. My body can't take any more pleasure. "Please, I don't think I can—"

He pulls out of me and wraps an arm around my waist before I can finish my sentence, twirling me around. I can't tell what is happening, but I feel him move my bound arms and hook them around his neck. His hands rest under my ass cheeks, parting my throbbing, dripping pussy. Suddenly, he lowers me onto his cock again.

I felt so empty without him inside me. This position penetrates me differently, hitting another pleasure center inside of me. It's so intense. Every nerve in my body lights on fire, and my blood starts to boil. I think he's trying to kill me.

"Fuck," I cry out, feeling the tears dampening the silk around my eyes.

Dante kisses me passionately, tangling his tongue with mine. His hands remain under my butt cheeks as he slowly moves me up and down his cock. "Keep your legs locked around me," he pants.

I do as he says, despite hardly having the energy.

Dante fucks me slower but with as much force, sending me

closer to the edge again. I never knew sex like this was even possible. I never knew you could have too much pleasure.

"I want your pretty little cunt to come all over my cock again, princess. Do you understand?"

I nod in response, too tired to speak.

"Be a good girl and come for daddy," he growls.

I focus on the pleasure that is ready to tear through me again, feeling the pressure as my muscles clamp around his cock. "Fuck, daddy," I cry out so loud, tumbling over the edge with such an explosion.

Dante bites my neck hard enough to hurt as he comes undone too. "Fuck," he growls as he unleashes his cum deep inside of me. I can feel it filling me up as he thrusts over and over again, draining every drop.

I turn limp in his arms, waiting for him to unbind me. The exhaustion spreading through me is like a disease. My eyes remain clamped shut under the blindfold, and I don't move. I'm not sure I have the energy to.

First, Dante unties the blindfold and pulls it away. I open my eyes, blinking quite a few times to get used to the light. He kisses me softly, eyes full of what looks like adoration. "You're so fucking perfect, Vi," he murmurs against my lips. "Lift your arms."

I struggle to lift my bound arms so that he can slip out of my hold. Once his support is gone, I fall back into the soft, plush bed. I can't move as I'm too tired. Dante gently unties the ropes around my wrists and allows me free. Still, I don't move.

The bed sinks next to me as he lies down, pulling me

toward him. He holds me against his chest tightly and kisses my forehead with a tenderness that is so contrasting to the rough, brutal fucking he just gave me. "Sleep now, princess," he murmurs, holding my head against his chest.

I do as he says, shutting my eyes. It doesn't take long for the pull of sleep to draw me into its warm, soothing cocoon

Dante's arms remain around me as I listen to his steady heartbeat beneath my head. I feel oddly safe, considering I'm lying in the arms of a wild beast.

16

DANTE

I wake with Violet nestled against me and feel an odd twinge in my chest. She looks stunning fast asleep in my arms, as though she belongs there. I grit my teeth, knowing that is a dangerous notion. My father insists I need a wife and children to solidify the Ortega Cartel's power and sustainability. He has a reason for arranging my marriage to someone I wouldn't care for because it makes me less vulnerable.

The alarm clock on the table tells me I'm late. Javier arranged a meeting at the office for nine o'clock, and its quarter to. The office is a half-hour drive at best.

I carefully pull my arm from under Violet not to wake her and gently get out of bed. She's still wearing the leather collar around her neck, and I don't ever want her to take it off. My name is etched into the leather, marking her as my property.

Violet didn't seem to mind my craving for dominating in

the bedroom, or if she did, she kept her mouth shut. Last night wasn't extreme, but I can't deny that I want to lock her in my sex room and never let her out. My addiction to this woman is a danger since my enemies have already tried to harm her.

I walk quietly out of her room and back to my bedroom, firing a text to Javier to let him know I'll be late. Quickly, I shower and get dressed before rushing out of my home.

Jorge is already waiting outside with the car, and he opens the back door for me. "Morning, sir."

"Morning," I reply, slipping into the back of the car.

I pull my phone out of my jacket and type in Violet's number. We took her phone when we kidnapped her, but I left it on the nightstand this morning. Now she's signed the non-disclosure agreement and contract. I'm confident she wouldn't betray me.

Morning, princess. Don't sleep all day.

I send the text and slip my phone back into my jacket, glancing out of the window as Jorge drives me to our office. After the attack on my property, no less, we need to find out what happened and who was behind it.

My phone buzzes, and I pull my cell phone out again. Violet's name is on the front, and I read her response.

I won't… Where are you, and how am I supposed to get this damn collar off?

I smile, knowing unless she asks Angela or another staff member to take it off for her, she has no chance.

Missing me already?

I fire my reply off, aware that it will irritate her.

Answer the questions.

I sigh, typing my reply.

A meeting and you never take the collar off. Do you understand?

She replies quickly.

No.

Her blatant disobedience grates on me. Violet knows I expect obedience as it was part of the contract she signed.

There will be serious consequences if you remove it. You are mine, and that collar is a symbol of my ownership. Do you understand?

I send my response, reiterating the question she gave a negative response to. Despite knowing Violet isn't yet entirely open to being submissive to me.

I see the bubbles ignite as she starts to type back. Then, they disappear. I wait, expecting the reply to come through. When it doesn't, I feel an irritation rising inside of me.

I asked you a question. Don't make me punish you when I return.

I focus on the area where the bubbles appear, but there's nothing after just under a minute. Violet wants me to punish her. I turn off the screen and set it to silent, putting it back into my pocket.

Jorge has got me to the office in record time as he pulls up the drop off point and gets out to open my door. "Shall I wait here for you, sir?" He asks.

I shake my head. "No, I'm not sure what time I'll be finished. I'll call you when I'm ready to leave."

He bows his head in answer, and I walk into the office. It's not unusual for me to be a little late, but more than half an hour is slack for me. No one would dare comment on my tardiness, but it's not acceptable since it's important to learn who attacked us.

Javier stands on the other side of the glass as I enter the office floor and open the door to the boardroom. Francisco, Ric, Javier, and Eduardo are sitting around the table, looking a little irritated.

I don't apologize to my lieutenants for being late. I never apologize. Instead, I walk to my seat at the head of the boardroom table and undo my suit jacket, shrugging it off and placing it on the back of the chair. Once I sit, it's only Ric that has the audacity to comment.

"Forget to set the alarm, Jefe?"

I glare at him and don't answer. "The attack in my grounds is an attack on the cartel."

Ric turns serious, and the rest of my lugartenientes look grave.

"It is. We need to burn the bastards behind it," Eduardo says.

I clear my throat. "First, we need to discover who was responsible. Any suggestions?"

There is silence. "No ideas at all?" I ask.

Javier sighs. "I've got a theory."

My attention moves to him. "Let me hear it."

He runs a hand through his hair. "Your father didn't take the news about your new fiancé well at all."

I sit up straighter, narrowing my eyes at him. "Are you suggesting my father arranged the hit on Violet?"

He shrugs. "It's too soon for any of our enemies to have learned that you're holding a woman you have feelings for captive."

I slam my hand down on the table. "Who said I have feelings for her?" It angers me that he would assume that since feelings are a sign of weakness.

Ric pipes in, "You've had a soft spot for that señorita since I can remember, boss. We're all friends here."

I clench my jaw and don't comment anymore on Javier's theory. If my father did try to kill Violet, we would have serious problems within our outfit. "Any other theories?"

Francisco clears his throat. "The only culprits for me are the Irish."

In my opinion, a more likely option, but I still can't understand why they attacked Violet.

I nod. "I agree. All of you need to get me concrete answers." I meet Javier's gaze. "Any news on the possible mole inside the outfit?"

Javier shakes his head. "Not yet, I have some theories, but I can't be sure."

"A mole?" Eduardo asks. He is often out of the loop since he deals with the business on a street-level most of the time.

I crack my neck. "Yeah, we've had some information leaks from inside of the cartel."

Francisco clenches his fists on the table. "When we find out who the traitor is, I'll break his fucking legs."

I shake my head. "Sorry amigo, but I'll be the one inflicting pain on the traitor," I say.

"That's not fair, keeping all the fun for yourself," Ric complains.

I shake my head. "Any other business to discuss?"

It's silent across the table, so I take that as a no. "I want answers to our problems, and I want them fast." I stand. "All of you put your heads together and get them for me."

"Boss," they all say in chorus.

I leave the room, and Javier follows me out. "Dante, I think you should speak to your father about the attack and your intention to marry an American."

I turn and meet his gaze, knowing that although my father is as ruthless as they come, I don't think he'd attack my woman. Even so, I can't rule it out. "I'll speak with him."

Javier nods. "I'll drop by the house once I have more information on the mole. I'm quietly confident but need to be sure."

I'm curious who he suspects, but don't question him as I don't want to know until he is certain. "See you later."

I don't wait for a reply, turning and pulling my cell phone out of my pocket. It angers me that there is still no response from Violet as I dial Jorge's number.

He picks up on the second dial tone. "I'll be there in ten minutes, boss."

"Thanks." I cancel the call and enter my office at our headquarters. I rarely spend time here, since I've got my office at home, which is more convenient.

A call to my father won't take long, and I'd rather do it here where people won't overhear. It's been a couple of months since we last spoke on the phone.

I open my contacts, and my finger hovers over his name. A moment of indecision plagues me before I start the call. The dial tone sounds five times before he picks up.

"Dante," he says.

I grit my teeth at his cold tone. "Father."

There are a few moments of silence. "What do you want?" he asks.

"Did you arrange a hit on my fiancé?" I know that there's no point engaging in small talk with him. He doesn't appreciate the small talk.

He doesn't respond at first, and that is all the answer I need. Javier was right. "You will not marry an American."

I feel rage flooding my veins. "You won't tell me who to marry, father. I'm my own man, and Violet will be my wife."

"¡Mira que cabrón." He tells me not to be a dumbass in Spanish—something that angers me more than I can put into words.

"If you don't stop your foolish attempt to stop me marrying her, I will be forced to strike back."

He clicks his tongue on the other end of the line. "You are foolish enough to believe I was behind it, but you don't look at who you wronged in the process of breaking your current engagement."

Gerardo Duarte.

"You are certain Duarte was behind this?"

I can sense my father's patience is wearing thin. "Don't question me. Gerardo was very unhappy when he learned that his daughter's fiancé had broken the engagement. It would be prudent to reconsider."

"Never," I respond, knowing that there's no chance I'd marry Rosa after Gerado tried to kill Violet. "I won't be intimidated by a low life drug producer."

"Do as you will. I won't be there to clear up your mess." He cancels the call without another word, leaving me staring at the wall.

He may have entrusted New York City's operations to me, but we both know he doesn't respect or trust my judgment. It's something that enrages me more than anything else can. I've proven myself to him time and time again, but I will always be the stupid little boy he raised in his eyes.

I stare at a bloodstain on the wall, feeling my rage taking on a life of its own. As it hits a peek, I growl and throw my cell phone at the wall. It smashes into pieces on the ground, but I don't care.

I will prove to my father that I'm more than capable of dealing with my problems. If Gerardo Duarte comes at me again, I'll make him wish he was never fucking born.

17

VIOLET

I've been pissed off all day because of Dante's stupid fucking order. He doesn't own me—no one does. I may have signed the contract, but that doesn't mean shit. It's illegal to own a person. It doesn't help that I'm also sore as hell after he fucked me like a beast more than once last night. Don't get me wrong, it was the best sex of my life, but it's also a reminder of the power he holds over me.

The collar around my neck is fucking embarrassing to wear, so I've put a turtleneck jumper on to hide it. There was no way in hell I was asking Angela to take it off me. I get the feeling that the look she would have given me might have killed me.

Thinking of Angela, I see her approaching me. "Dinner is served in the dining room, and your presence is requested."

I stare at her blankly. "I'm not dressed for dinner."

"Too bad. The boss's orders." She nods down the corridor toward the dining room. "Off you go."

Dinner the other night was because he wanted to discuss his proposal, and I haven't been invited since.

Why would he want to have dinner with me?

Dante probably hated me ignoring his last texts, asking me if I understood not to take the collar off. Lucky for him, I didn't have any way of taking it off other than trying to cut it. I had the feeling that cutting it off would be a bad idea.

I walk toward the dining room, glancing back briefly at Angela. She's watching me with eagle eyes, making sure I do as I'm told. At times, it feels like I'm a child the way I'm treated here. I guess I better get used to it.

The door to the dining room is cracked open, and I walk inside. Dante is sitting at the head of a ridiculously long table. The room is enormous and cold—different from the office we dined in before.

I clear my throat. "You wanted to see me?"

His gaze lifts from his plate and meets mine. The cold, ruthless look in his eyes scares me and excites me all at the same time. "Come here." His order is direct and full of warning.

I walk toward him, feeling irritated by his blatant lack of respect for me. "What is this about?"

He stands, striding over to me fast. He grabs hold of my hips and pulls me close to him, pulling down the collar of my turtleneck. "I want to check that you did as I said," he growls. He reveals the leather collar that I've worn all day. "Good." He grabs the bottom of the jumper and forces it over my head, leaving me in only a thin shirt underneath and no bra. My breasts are visible through the thin white fabric. He let's go of me and takes a step back, eyes fixed on my hard nipples. "Why didn't you respond to my question?"

I hold his gaze, not allowing him to intimidate me. "It didn't need an answer."

The hardness in his gaze is almost cruel. "Every question I ask you needs an answer, Violet. Do you understand?"

My nature doesn't allow me to accept this is now my life, reduced to nothing more than a servant. When it comes to the bedroom it's a turn on, but any other time it's irritating. "No, I don't."

Dante growls, eyes frantic as he grabs me and pushes me into a seat at the table, caging me in with hands placed on each arm of the chair. "You signed a contract, Violet. Did you not understand the terms?"

I nod. "I understood the terms fine, but you said you want to convince me to marry you in two months. Are you telling me this is what I should expect?"

He leans closer to me, baring his teeth like an angry dog. "Yes, I expect you to learn to obey me as my wife."

"Well, I'm afraid you will be disappointed." I lift my chin in a sign of defiance. "You will have my obedience in the bedroom as set out in the contract, but not in my day-to-day life."

Dante's nostrils flare, but he pushes away from me and returns to his chair. The tension is so thick it feels like it's starving the oxygen from the air. I'm not sure what to expect next.

"Eat," he orders.

I look at the table laden with expensive food and don't feel hungry at all. "I'm not hungry." I cross my arms over my chest, knowing he may try to force me to eat.

He stands, knocking his chair to the floor with a crash. Dante walks over to me like a predator stalking its prey. Quickly, he grabs the back of my neck and forces me to look into his eyes. "I'm going to punish you for your disobedience, princess." With his other hand, he unzips his pants and frees his huge cock.

I stare at it in shock, wondering if he'd get me to suck him off in the dining room. Any of the staff could walk in.

"Open," he orders, staring down at me with that cold, hard gaze.

I do as he says, opening my mouth. My eagerness annoys the rational part of my brain, but my body ignores all rational. I want to suck his cock and taste him again.

Slowly, he slips inch after inch into the back of my throat, making me gag.

"You may not be hungry for food, Vi, but I know you are starving for daddy's cock."

I look up at him and meet his gaze, noticing the heat in his expression. All I can do is focus on breathing through my nose, trying to stop myself from gagging. Dante starts to thrust in and out of my throat slowly, giving me time to get used to the invasion of his cock pushing past my gag reflex.

I knew it was only a matter of time until he started to increase the tempo, and I was right. Saliva spills from my mouth all over the thin shirt I'm wearing, making it more see-through.

Dante plays with my nipples with one hand as he holds the back of my head with the other. "You're a naughty fucking girl, Vi, disobeying me the way you have today."

I moan around his cock as I keep all my focus on breathing through my nose.

"Naughty girls get punished. Do you understand?" He slips his cock out of my mouth to allow me to respond.

"Yes, daddy," I reply, no longer feeling the need to disobey him. I'm too overcome with desire. My clit throbs with need as I rock back and forth in the chair, trying to get friction.

He grabs hold of my wrists with the hand and pulls me off his cock. "You're a naughty slut for trying to get off like that." He lifts me out of the chair by my wrists and grabs my ass cheeks in his hands, pulling me firm against him. "Only daddy gets you off, princess."

"Sorry, daddy," I say. Finding my obedient nature comes easily the moment we enter these roles. "I'm just so horny," I say, batting my eyelids at him.

He growls and presses his lips to mine, forcing his tongue into my mouth as he takes everything from me. I turn limp, allowing him to dominate me in every way. The power he has over me is both intoxicating and infuriating. I've spent all day pissed at him, but the moment his hands are on me, I'm his submissive slut, begging for more.

Dante unbuttons my jeans and pulls down the zip, forcing them roughly down my hips. His eyes move down to the lacy red thong I'm wearing. "You're fucking perfect, princess."

He lifts me off the ground as if I weigh nothing and sets me down on a clear part of the enormous solid wood dining table. "I'm going to fuck you so hard all the staff will hear you being my good little girl," he growls into my ear.

I shudder, knowing that he isn't bluffing.

He cups my pussy in his hand, making the need inside of me grow. "This is mine and only mine."

I watch as he hooks a finger into the knot of his tie and undoes it, flattening the fabric and tying it around my eyes. Part of me feels disappointed that I won't be able to watch as he fucks me hungrily. Another part of me knows how everything feels better when one of your senses is removed entirely.

Suddenly, I feel him tear away my panties, and then his tongue probes at my throbbing clit.

"Fuck," I cry out, gripping the side of the table for support.

"Hands behind your back, and don't move them, princess."

I reluctantly do as he says, keeping my hands behind me. All I want to do is run them through his dark, cropped hair and touch every inch of him. It's so perverse that I want a man who has kidnapped me. The man who has left me no choice but to be his submissive.

His mouth returns to my pussy, and all thoughts float away. My head falls back as I moan softly, accepting the way he makes me feel. He makes me feel like I'm walking on clouds every time he touches me. "Yes, daddy," I moan as he thrusts two thick fingers inside of me.

He nibbles on my neck, sending waves of pleasure crashing

through me. I forget where we are and what we are doing. "You need to prove you can be a good girl."

I bite my lip, trying to stop myself from moaning too loud.

His fingers leave me, and the zip of his pants coming undone makes me freeze. Suddenly, something far larger presses against my slick, aching opening. Dante drags his cock through me before grabbing my hips roughly and flipping me onto all fours.

He spanks my ass. "Next time, you answer me when I ask you a question, princess." He spanks me again and again, doling out his punishment.

Every impact makes me needier for his cock. I arch my back, wanting him to fuck me more than anything I've wanted in my life. "Fuck me, daddy," I beg.

He stops spanking me and grabs hold of my hair, yanking me backward. His lips tease at my ear. "Should naughty girls get what they want?" he asks.

I shake my head. "No, but you've punished me enough," I whine.

He bites the lobe of my ear softly. "Is that right, princess?"

"Yes, daddy." I arch my back, desperate to have him inside of me. "Please give me your cock."

He doesn't say another word, sliding every inch of his hard, throbbing cock inside of me.

I cry out, loving the way my muscles stretch to accommodate his huge size.

Dante grabs one of my wrists and pins it behind my back, leaving me resting on one arm on the hard table. He starts to fuck me in and out with deep, rhythmic strokes, making the china on the table rattle with each thrust.

Almost instantly, I feel the pressure building within. Dante increases the tempo, pounding into me harder and faster with each stroke until the table is rocking.

I gasp as I hear a smash and plates start to fall from the table to the floor. I try to claw myself away from Dante in a panic. "Stop, people will come in," I shout.

Dante spanks me. "No, they won't, princess. I ordered Angela to lock the door after you came in and ensure no one enters under any circumstance," he growls, fucking me even harder.

It shouldn't surprise me that the invite to dinner was a disguise for wanting to punish me. This was his plan. He takes me hard, not caring as more china smashes onto the ground with the force of his assault on me.

"I want to feel that tight little cunt come on daddy's cock," Dante growls from behind me, holding my wrist so tight I think he's cutting off the blood flow.

His other hand digs into my hip possessively and most certainly will leave bruises as he takes me like a wild animal. I feel myself coming apart before he's even ordered me to.

"That's it, princess, come for me," he growls.

"Fuck, yes," I scream, stars filtering my vision as my body begins to spasm. Every muscle tightens, and every nerve ending lights up.

His cock seems to get even harder as he fucks me through my orgasm before roaring as he comes undone too. It feels like forever passes between us as we stay in the same position, panting for breath. Dante keeps his still rock-hard cock deep inside of me all the while.

I can't believe how easily he can flip me from pissed as hell at him to begging him for his cock. Every time that Dante takes me in hand so roughly, I get a little more hooked on him.

PEDRO LOOKS up as I enter the hospital wing of Dante's home. When I first discovered there was a hospital in his house, I thought it very odd. Pedro explained the reason to me. None of Dante's men can go to a normal hospital if involved in a shooting because of the questions it will raise.

He smiles, shaking his head. "When are you going to let me rest in peace?"

I hold up a container of brownies I stole from the kitchen. "I have brownies."

He laughs. "If Dante knew how often you visited me, I'd be in big fucking trouble."

I set the brownies down on the side table and dig out a book. "You're in here because you saved my life. I owe you baked goods and a bit of company every day." I shrug. "It would be rude otherwise."

Little does Pedro know that my visits to him are often the highlight of my day lately. It's been a week and a half since the attack, and he's the only person who talks to me in this damn place. All of the staff are stuck up their asses, especially Angela.

"Same book?" he asks.

I nod. "We're near the end of the story."

"Thank fuck for that."

I raise a brow. "Are you telling me you aren't intrigued by how Moby Dick ends?"

He shakes his head. "It's alright, but a bit depressing. I wish you'd picked something with a bit of romance in."

I raise an eyebrow, surprised by the sentiment.

He shrugs, wincing a little at the action. "What? I'm a softy under it all."

I can't help but laugh. The only time I laugh anymore is with Pedro. Dante may have given me my phone back, but he's blocked all outgoing calls and numbers I regularly contacted. It means I can never contact my friends like Alice, who I lived and worked with. She probably thinks I'm dead in a ditch.

"It's lucky I bought Pride and Prejudice with me then, isn't it?" I ask, pulling out the book.

He pulls a face. "You've got to be kidding me. I meant some steamy, hot romance, not that period crap."

I laugh. "How about we just talk today then?"

He relaxes into the bed. "Sounds good to me." He sighs heavily, resting his head back and shutting his eyes. "How has your day been so far?" he asks.

I shrug. "Pretty boring, to be honest. The highlights of my day are visiting you."

He raises a brow. "Damn, you need to get out more, señorita."

I swallow hard. "I would if I were allowed to."

Pedro sits up straighter, looking at me with a puzzled expression. "You've been banned from walking the grounds?"

"Yes, ever since the attack I've been stuck inside." My brow furrows. "A bit like you, I guess."

He smiles sadly. "I'm sorry about that. They must believe you were the intended target then." He tilts his head. "Are you someone important?"

"Not that I'm aware of." It falls silent between us as Pedro continues to look puzzled.

"What is your relationship with Dante, if you don't mind me asking?"

I feel my cheeks heat as that's a difficult question to answer. Our relationship is complicated. "I saw something I wasn't meant to see, as I told you." I hope he might get the gist that I don't want to talk about it.

"Yes, but normally if there's a witness to a crime, that witness has to be wiped out. So, why were you spared?"

I feel the heat spreading down my neck. "Because Dante has a soft spot for me, I believe."

Pedro nods. "Yeah, I know you have been sleeping with him, but he must care for you to keep you around."

My stomach churns at those words. If Dante cares for me, he sure as hell doesn't show it. "Not sure that's true."

"What do I know? I've not known him long, but his reputation proceeds him. He doesn't ever keep a woman around for long." He sighs and rests back in the bed. "I hope he keeps you around, though. You're a good one."

I smile at that and open the container of brownies. "Brownie?"

"I thought you would never ask." He plucks one from the container, laughing.

I nibble at one of them, thinking about Pedro's words. Dante can't care for me. He shows no signs of having any real interest in getting to know me. "Dante is dangerous, isn't he?"

Pedro tenses a little. "What do you mean?"

"I mean, he's not the kind of man any girl wants to take home to meet their mom. If they had one, that is." I shrug. "I guess that doesn't matter for me."

Sadness claws at me as I haven't thought about my mom for a while. Anytime I do, I feel myself slipping back into despair.

"No, he's not. What happened to your mom?"

I shake my head. "Cancer."

He grabs my hand and squeezes softly. "I'm sorry, Violet."

I nod and squeeze his hand back, thankful for the easy friendship I've found with someone here. It does surprise me that it turned out to be my bodyguard, but life is unpredictable nowadays. I've given up trying to guess what will happen next.

DANTE

I walk toward the lake, needing space to clear my head. Violet won't come down here, not since I've banned her from walking the grounds. Once I knew Duarte was possibly trying to carry out a hit on her, I banned her from leaving the house entirely.

I would go to any length to protect her, but Javier has had my men trying to find answers to who the attacker was for just under two weeks, and we've got nothing. There hasn't been another attack, but I know it's only a matter of time.

My feelings for Violet are dangerous, but I know I can't deny the truth any longer.

I love her.

Even before she witnessed the monster I truly am, I loved her. It's why I should never have kept her alive once she witnessed me kill Miguel, but also how I knew I would never be able to take her life—no matter what.

My father has no capacity for love, and he expects the same from his son. He's ruthless and cold-hearted, and if he knew I'd fallen for her, then he would go out of his way to end her life.

A man with something to lose is a weak man.

I can hear him saying those words to me in my mind over and over again. There have been times when I've looked at Violet and desperately wanted to tell her the truth—tell her how much I love her.

Once those words are spoken, they can't be taken back. It's been two weeks since the attack on Violet's life here at the side of this lake. I stare at the bullet holes in the tree they'd hidden behind, feeling so angry.

Pedro saved her life, and for that, I'll always owe him a debt I couldn't repay. I can't deny that her daily visits to see him have awoken a jealousy inside of me that is uncharacteristic, even though I know it's innocent enough. They have bonded over the incident, and I get the feeling Violet gets lonely here. I don't exactly provide her much company.

All I do is take what I need from her, dominating her over and over again, then leave. I can't help it. Anytime I try to engage in conversation with her, my mind reminds me of the danger she poses if I get too close. I know it's too late. She's already my addiction.

We are over two weeks into our arrangement, but I know any amount of time with her won't be enough. I want Violet forever, but I'm not doing a great job convincing her to be my wife.

"Boss," Ric calls down to me as he jogs along the path to the lake. "I've been looking everywhere for you."

"What's up?"

He runs a hand across the back of his neck. "Javier sent me to find you and tell you he found the mole in our outfit for sure."

I raise a brow, wondering why Javier hasn't come to me directly. "Who is it?"

He looks at the ground, not making eye contact with me. "Javier found evidence that Eduardo is the one behind the leak."

"Eduardo?" I ask, surprised by his findings since he's always been a loyal warrior for the Ortega Cartel. "Does he know who he's working for?"

Ric shakes his head. "He says so, but he didn't tell me who he's working for. Javier wanted me to update you."

"Why didn't Javier come and tell me this himself?"

"He's got a meeting with Eduardo right now, so sent me to let you know what is going on." He shakes his head. "I'm surprised Eduardo would stoop so low."

I pull my cell phone out of my jacket and dial Javier's number. "Jefe?"

"Don't interrogate him without me. Where are you?"

There are a few moments of silence. "The office, boss."

I grit my teeth and cancel the call, feeling irritated that Javier had the nerve to consider meeting with the mole without me present. "I'm going to the office. Call Jorge and ask him to get the car ready."

Ric nods. "On it, jefe." He makes the call as we walk back toward the main house. This is what I need right now to get my mind off of the woman I can't stop thinking about. If Eduardo has been working for the Irish, I'll make sure he pays the ultimate price for his betrayal.

ADRENALINE PULSES through my veins as I enter the office. Ric follows close behind. I see Javier sitting in the boardroom with Eduardo. They are talking together as if nothing is wrong. Javier must have got the hint from my call that I don't want him to do anything until I'm present. Matters like this always have to be dealt with by the boss.

I open the door to the boardroom. "Javier. A word."

Javier stands and follows me. Once the door is shut and we're out of earshot, I speak, "Are you sure it's Eduardo?"

He reaches into his inside jacket pocket and pulls out some photos of Eduardo sitting down with Devlin Murphy himself. "Bastardo," I growl, clenching my fists by my side. "How long do you suspect he's been feeding information?"

Javier grits his teeth, looking uncertain about answering the question. "You won't like the answer, jefe."

I shake my head. "I don't care if I like it or not. How long, Javier?"

"Two years, I believe. Phone records show Eduardo has been in touch with Devlin ever since he landed the position as your lieutenant after Juan's death."

Two fucking years.

It sounds about right since that's when the Irish started gaining ground on us. "Motherfucker. I'm going to make him wish he was never born. Do you think he had a hand in Juan's death?" Even two years later, we've yet to find out who planted the hit on him. It will make sense if Eduardo has been covering it up.

Javier nods. "It's possible."

I barge back into the boardroom and slam my hands down on the desk. "It would be best if you come clean now to me, Eduardo," I growl.

His eyes widen, and I notice his dark complexion pale. "Sir?"

"Don't sir me," I growl, walking toward him and grabbing him by his stupid fucking tie. "You have been feeding inside information to the fucking idiot of an Irishman for two damn years."

Eduardo shakes his head. "I-I don't know what you are talking about, jefe."

I let go of his tie and signal for Javier to enter the room. "Show him the photos we have."

Javier chucks them down in front of Eduardo, and he pales more.

"I can explain. It's not what it looks like."

I raise a brow as I've heard it all before. Every time a traitor gets caught, he always begs for his life and tries to twist the evidence. "Save it, Eduardo. We've got other evidence."

His Adam's apple bobs as he swallows hard. "Fine. Let me have it," he says.

I'm surprised he gave up so easily, but Eduardo has

witnessed what I do to traitors on many occasions. He knows that arguing his case will only make it worse for him. I glance at Ric, who pulls out my torture instruments in a black briefcase.

He sets it on the table and opens it. I want to inflict as much pain as possible before I end his life. Eduardo has caused us so much grief, and I want to know if he did kill Juan.

I grab a pair of pliers and put it around his first fingernail. Eduardo tries to pull away, but Ric sets his hands on his shoulders. "Don't move," he growls.

"Now, I want to know if you had a hand in getting rid of your predecessor."

Eduardo's brow furrows. "What?"

I force the pressure onto his nail and start to tear it off of him. He squeals like a fucking girl as I rip the nail from his flesh. "Fuck," he shouts, shaking his head frantically.

"Jefe, would you let me have a go?" Javier asks.

I pass the pliers to him and take his place behind Eduardo, knowing that he was seriously close to Juan. If Eduardo had anything to do with his death, Javier would want a piece of the action. I'm one of the only people in this world that knows the truth about my lieutenant—Javier. He prefers men, and Juan was his lover, which isn't widely accepted within the world that we operate in. Only the band knows the truth about him, and it will always remain that way.

"Tell us the truth about Juan. Did you kill him?" he asks, keeping the pliers around the next nail on his hand.

Eduardo swallows, meeting Javier's gaze. "I helped Devlin plan it, yes."

Javier growls like an animal, ripping the nail from his finger so fast Eduardo doesn't expect it. He howls in pain, tears flooding his eyes.

"Jefe, I need permission to take his life slowly and painfully," Javier says calmly.

I know that it's what my loyal and faithful lugarteniente needs and deserves. He really loved Juan and I won't take the revenge away from him. "Of course. First, let me give Eduardo a parting gift." I walk toward him and grab his chin between my finger and thumb hard. "You made a mistake choosing to side with the Irish. I don't know why a coward like you would betray his people, and I don't fucking care. You are dead to the cartel." I punch him hard in the nose, breaking it. I meet Javier's gaze. "Make sure he suffers a slow and painful death, compañero."

"You don't need to tell me." The rage in Javier's eyes is unlike anything I've seen in them before. He's out for revenge, even though I know that path won't make it hurt any less.

Ric steps forward. "Do you want me to stay, or you want to go this one alone?"

Javier looks up at Ric. "Stay. You won't want to miss this show."

I clap Javier on the shoulder. "I'll see you all soon. I hope you rot in hell, Eduardo." With that, I walk away from my men and allow them to deal with the traitor. Normally, I'd torture him myself, but Javier needs the opportunity for closure, even if it won't bring Juan back.

All I hear are tortured screams as I head out of the office and back down to the street. I smile to myself, thankful that we've finally found the leak in our organization. Devlin may think he's clever, but now he doesn't have an inside man, I'd like to see him stop our expansion without a mole feeding him information.

VIOLET

I signed the contract binding me to the man I'm inexplicably taken with three weeks ago. After he kidnapped me, I should feel nothing but hate for him. Instead, all I feel is adoration for a man who has snatched away my free will.

He uses me as he wants and then leaves. Often, he hardly says a word to me. I wonder if he's changed his mind about convincing me to marry him.

Does he believe that the mind-blowing sex is enough?

The sex is better than anything I've experienced before. Each time Dante pushes the boundaries a little more, restraining me with more rope, bringing out a paddle to spank me, and even gagging me with a ball gag. Something tells me he's still holding back. Dante's tastes are dark and twisted, and yet I love it.

I can't tell whether he's holding back to protect me or

because he's too scared to reveal his desires to me entirely. Dante has been colder and more distant since we've been having sex than he ever was with me at the bar. It makes little sense. We may be crossing that line into intimacy, but all the easy flirting has gone. It's as though this is merely a transaction to him.

The contract mentioned he wants a woman to give him children. If I were to agree to marry him at the end of the two months, he'd want me pregnant. It makes me feel like all I'd be to him is a prized bitch ready to be bred from. He doesn't want to get to know me personally, and that's why I know I can't agree, no matter how much I care for him.

Pedro is almost fully recovered and will be getting out of the hospital in a couple of days, but I go to see him every day still. I think I worry him, as he knows if Dante were to suspect there was anything more than friendship between us, he'd probably finish what the attackers started.

I walk through the corridors, heading toward the library— my favorite room. Reading is a passion of mine that I've hardly had time for with work. Dante has thousands of books gathering dust, so I hide out in there now all day, every day.

I open the door to the library and gasp in surprise when I see Dante sitting on the couch, reading.

Dante looks up at me, meeting my gaze. "Are you lost, princess?"

I shake my head. "No, I spend my time in here most days since I discovered this place," I say, shutting the door behind me and approaching him cautiously. "Is that a problem?"

Dante shakes his head. "No, I just like to get away at times in here." He pats the space next to him on the sofa. "Come and join me."

The look in his eyes tells me he doesn't want to chat, but I can't help the reluctance clawing at me. I need to talk to him about my concerns, no matter what reaction I might face.

I sit down, and he reaches for me. "Dante, wait."

He tilts his head to the side but doesn't say anything.

"I want to talk to you about something."

His dark eyes turn a little cold as he shifts uncomfortably on the sofa. "What?" The tone of his voice is suddenly hard.

"Why are you so distant?" I ask.

He stands, and my stomach sinks. I'm sure he doesn't intend to answer me, running away from the question. "It's complicated," he says, walking toward a shelf and placing his book back onto it.

I swallow hard, wondering if he's about to walk out on me like he always does. Instead, he turns and rejoins me on the sofa.

My heart skips a beat as he takes my hand in his and looks into my eyes.

"I'm sorry you feel I've been distant." He shakes his head. "When my enemy attacked you, I realized the dangerous position I had put myself in."

My brow furrows. "I don't understand."

He pinches the bridge of his nose, looking stressed. "I've got something to lose now. You," he breathes, meeting my gaze intently.

"You barely speak to me. I doubt my loss would bother you that much."

He growls, wrapping a hand around my throat hard. "You have no idea how much you mean to me, princess."

I can hardly breathe, but I manage to speak. "You have a funny way of showing it."

He moves his face closer to mine, searching my eyes. "I can't be vulnerable, but you… You make me vulnerable." He lets go of my throat, and I draw in a breath. "I'm the head of my family's cartel here in New York, and if I care for you then…" He trails off as if he has said too much. "Maybe this was a mistake."

I can feel him pulling away from me when he was close to opening up for the first time. I reach for his face and gently cup his cheek. "It's not a mistake. We're not a mistake."

He holds my gaze. For the first time, it feels like I can see into his soul. The dark and twisted soul that he tries to hide from me. His lips descend on mine hungrily. When we part, we're both panting for air.

He rests his forehead against mine. "You're everything to me," he breathes.

I feel my chest ache at the rawness in his voice. "I love you, Dante." I don't mean to say it, but it just slips out. It's the truth. Before he even kidnapped me, I loved him. Our weekly chats before his band played were always the highlight of my week.

He tenses against me, and as if a switch flicks, he turns cold again. "Lie down," he orders.

I do as he says but feel the ache in my chest at his dismissal. He kisses me passionately, his tongue delving inside of my mouth. For the first time, I'm free to wrap my arms around his neck, so I do. I run my hands through his short-cropped hair, moaning as his hard cock presses between my legs.

I'm surprised at the gentleness of his touch as he pulls away and cups my breasts in his hands. "You're so beautiful," he says, bringing his lips to my exposed cleavage. "I want you naked." He seems to have forgotten my declaration of love as the passion between us ignites.

He unbuttons my shirt and pulls it open, groaning as my bare breasts are revealed to him. "No bra?" he murmurs.

I shrug. "It's more comfortable without it."

He groans and sucks on my left nipple first, sending shock waves of pleasure radiating between my legs. I feel myself getting wetter and wetter as he moves to the right nipple. There's a tenderness in his touch as he moves lower toward my pants, trailing kisses down my stomach.

Dante pops open the button on my pants and pulls the zip down. "No panties either?" he asks, looking up at me.

Lately, I haven't bothered with them as they've been getting in the way whenever he comes to me and ravages me like a beast. He pulls my pants off of me, leaving me naked.

Dante stands and takes a step back, towering over me. His eyes rake over every inch of me, standing dressed in a tight shirt and jeans. The press of his hard cock visible against the denim. He kneels on the couch and kisses each of my thighs, making me tremble with anticipation. Slowly, he drags his tongue to the apex of my thighs and drags it through my soaking wet folds.

My hips buck at the pleasure, having him tasting me there.

His tongue moves from tasting me to my clit as he turns me into a molten puddle beneath him. "Dante," I breathe his name.

He thrusts two fingers inside my dripping wet pussy and lavishes all his attention on my clit, licking and sucking it in a way that sends me higher than the fucking clouds. I can't believe how quick he can bring me to orgasm, and this time he doesn't toy with me. He allows me to come instantly, not letting up.

As my pussy gushes with juice, he laps up every drop. "Sweet as fucking sin, princess," he murmurs.

He unzips his pants and frees his cock through the flies of his jeans. I lick my lips at the sight of his hard cock, dripping with precum. The desire to taste him overwhelms me.

"Are you going to fuck my throat, daddy?" I ask.

He groans. "Is that what you want?"

I nod in response, wanting nothing more than to taste him. He places his thighs on either side of my head, and his heavy cock nudges at my lips. "Open up for me, princess."

I do as he says, and he thrusts every inch deep into the back of my throat. The force makes me gag, but I gain control of my reflexes, allowing him to slip in and out of my throat at a steady rhythm.

He grunts like an animal as his cock leaks down my throat. Saliva spills all over me and his thighs as he fucks my throat like it's my pussy. I'm so wet between my thighs, aching to feel him fill me to the hilt.

He pulls out after a while, panting for breath. "I need to fuck you, princess before I cum down your throat."

I lick my lips. "You know I love swallowing your cum, daddy," I moan, batting my eyelashes at him.

He growls softly. "I do, princess, but right now, I want my cock buried inside your pussy."

I watch as he moves back and puts one leg on the floor and the other on the couch, positioning his hard cock at my entrance. Tremors of anticipation pulse through me as I long for him more than anything.

Dante holds my gaze, and the intensity in his eyes makes me shiver. It's something that until now I've been robbed of seeing, always blindfolded or forced onto my knees so I can't see him. The intimacy of it makes me shudder as he slowly drags the tip of his cock through my soaking wet entrance.

"Are you ready for my cock, princess?"

I lick my lips and nod, feeling that ache for him deep inside of me.

He pushes forward with one hard thrust, slipping every inch through my tight entrance. I gasp as my muscles stretch to welcome him, tightening around him as if they never want him to leave.

I wrap my arms around his neck and pull him close, and he allows me to. It's the first time I've been free to touch him, and I'm not letting the opportunity go to waste. "Take off your shirt," I gasp.

He raises a brow. "Remember who is in charge, Vi."

I nod. "I know, but I want to touch you, please, daddy." I bat my eyelashes, hoping he will take it off.

He pulls his shirt over his head and tosses it to the side, revealing his muscled chest with a dark tattoo on his right pectoral. I run my hands over him, feeling the short dark hair that covers his skin. There's a large scar on his stomach the disappears into the waistband of his pants, which he still has on. I wonder how he got it, but I know it's not the time to ask.

Dante kisses me gently, surprising me by the way his tongue softly demands entrance into my mouth. He moves in and out of me with deep but tender thrusts, making love to me. This is the gentlest he's been with me, and while I love his rough and dominant side, right now, this is what I need.

I've opened myself up to Dante and told him I love him because it's true. It's as though he knows that being rough with me now might break me.

He knows the power he holds over me. One wrong move, and he could crush my heart easily. I hope he never hurts me, but I feel so vulnerable to the darkness that lies inside of the man taking me so gently.

20

DANTE

*A*ll my control slips through my fingers as I ravage the woman beneath me. At first, I was gentle, but nothing about me is gentle.

Every thrust of my cock is harder than the last. I can't let Violet's words get to me. Love is weak, and it's not something I should indulge in, even though I know it's too late.

The danger, which is a part of my life, means love only gives you something to lose. My father taught me that when he shot my mother in front of my eyes. It was to prove to my sister and me that love is a weakness. One that your enemies can use against you.

Violet has managed to infect my cold, dark heart. It doesn't only prove dangerous to me but her as well.

Violet moans as I flip her onto her front and press her hard into the couch, wishing I had my restraints to bind her. For the first time, my control has snapped, and I've taken her like this.

Her profession of love both scared me and turned me on. It makes no sense.

"Harder, daddy," she moans.

Fuck.

This girl loves it so damn rough. I've never known anyone take my cock the way she does, begging for it like a fucking whore. "You're such a good little slut, begging daddy for it hard," I pant, spanking her ass hard with my palm.

She cries out, arching her back. "Please, daddy, fuck me harder."

All control slips as I start to take her without mercy. Our bodies come together in a hard, frantic clash of flesh against flesh. She moans louder, neither of us caring that the library is open to anyone walking in at any moment. We're both consumed by our passion for one another—a passion I've been trying to keep strictly sexual.

My coldness hasn't kept Violet from falling for me. If anything, it's made her fall harder. It was a mistake to offer her that contract.

The fire between us was never merely based on sexual desire, and I knew that. It has always been deeper. Violet digs her fingertips into my back as I continue to passionately fuck her into the couch, feeling myself getting closer and closer to exploding inside of her.

"Dante," she moans my name as I drive her higher. Normally, I'd punish her and tell her to call me daddy when we fuck, but right now, I'm not in that headspace—right now, I'm making love to my woman. I flip her back onto her back and grab her breast in my hand, playing with her hard nipple.

I capture her lips and kiss her as I fuck her harder, feeling the strength of my emotions overwhelm me. Our tongues tangle together as I feel her pussy tighten around me, warning me that she's close to coming undone.

It's too soon for her to come. I need to feel her come at the same time as me, so I still inside of her. It earns me a frustrated whimper. "Don't stop," she breathes.

I kiss her lips again. "I need you to come when I tell you, princess." I move in and out of her slowly, looking into her eyes as I make love to her.

It's the first time I've allowed our sexual encounter to escape my normal desire to control every aspect. Me fucking Violet in the library was spontaneous and passionate. Our lovemaking is proof that Violet means more to me than any woman I've ever met. No matter how badly I want to deny it, I know that I'm in love with the woman beneath me.

Tenderness isn't something that comes easily to me, but for Violet, it seems I'm capable of being gentler. I dig my teeth into her collarbone softly, making her moan. Her desire and tolerance for pain during sex is proof that we were meant to find each other.

She claws at my back, sinking her nails in hard enough to hurt. It increases my pleasure as we move as one, our souls coming together in a mating that transcends all the barriers I've carefully erected around my heart, mind, and soul. I feel a deep connection inside of me to her that both moves and scares me.

"Dante," she moans my name, and it's like music to my ears.

I kiss her lips again, drowning in the intensity of my feelings for her. Somehow, this beauty has managed to unlock the small amount of light that survives under the crushing darkness inside of me. "I want you to come for me, mi amor," I breathe into her ear.

Her pussy muscles tighten around me, drawing me deeper inside of her. "Fuck," she cries out, her thighs quivering as the intensity of her orgasm hits her.

I come right along with her, growling as I release every drop of my seed deep inside of her. Mine. Violet is all mine, forever and always. I don't stop until every drop of my seed is emptied deep inside of her.

Her eyes are shut as she lies beneath me, panting for breath. Her hair is messy and beautiful, and the expression on her face is one of pure bliss. An image I want to hold onto forever. I knew before I kidnapped Violet that this was never going to be just about sex. She is my world and has been for two years.

I WAKE the next morning as my new cell phone rings. Vi is sleeping, turned over with her back to me. The first time she has slept in my room. It's the first time I've ever had any woman sleep in my space. I expected it to feel weird, but it feels natural.

"Hello," I say, picking up the phone.

"You sound like you've just woken up. It's almost ten in the morning where you are."

My father's voice puts me on edge. He never calls me. "What's wrong?"

"I've been given a tip that Duarte intends to attack the woman you've got engaged to again."

My attention moves to Violet, who is staring at me now, sleepily. I woke her.

"Do you know when?" I ask.

My father sighs heavily. "Not exactly, but soon I believe. Be vigilant is all I'm telling you."

I'm surprised he rang me since her death would suit him. "Why did you decide to warn me?"

"Because you are my son, and Javier believes you care for the woman." There's a hint of disapproval in his tone. "I can't say I'm happy that you weren't more careful, but it is what it is." There's a short pause.

"Thank you for warning me."

"It's nothing." He cancels the call without a goodbye, but the call in itself is more than I'd expect from my father.

"Is everything okay?" Violet asks, sitting up in the bed. It's impossible to keep my eyes off her exposed breasts as the sheet falls from her. Instantly, I'm distracted from the terrible news I've been given. "Dante?" She looks a little concerned.

"Sorry, I got distracted by your amazing breasts."

She looks down and pulls the duvet up, flushing. Which is adorable considering all the things I've done to her. "You sounded worried on the phone."

I sit next to her on the bed, scrubbing a hand across the back of my neck. "It was my father."

She sits up a little straighter. "What did he want?"

It would be dangerous not to tell her the truth, especially if Duarte has a hit out on her. "He wanted to warn me about a threat." I take her hand. "As I mentioned before, my father had arranged my wedding to a Mexican woman I'd never met."

She nods slowly in response.

"Her father has a hit out on you. We believe he was behind the first attempt on your life." I sigh heavily. "Let's just say he wasn't happy about my decision not to marry his daughter."

She pulls her hand from mine, and her face pales. "They are going to try again?"

I hate the fear in her voice. This was the kind of danger I always protected her from by not making a move at the bar. Until the night she witnessed that murder, and I'd slipped up while we were alone in Carlos's office.

"Yes." I slip my arm around her shoulders and pull her close. "Don't worry. I'll keep you safe."

She tenses, pulling away from me. "Do you mean you will keep me locked up in this house forever?"

I grit my teeth. "Would you rather be shot dead outside?"

She folds her arms over her chest defensively. "No, but I can't stay locked in here forever."

"You have to understand the danger. My father wanted me to marry the Mexican woman he chose because I wouldn't care for her. She would merely be my wife by arrangement, and I wouldn't have anything to lose."

She meets my gaze. "But now you have something to lose?"

I clench my jaw, knowing she wants me to tell her the truth

that I love her too. It's difficult for me to utter those words, which I've never said to another human being. "Yes. My enemies can use you against me, Violet."

"So, because you might lose me, it's best I'm miserable for the rest of my life locked in a fucking tower. Is that right?" She shakes her head, standing and walking away from me. "There's no certainty in any aspect of life, Dante. Whether you're a criminal or a fucking post-man, shit happens, and you have to live with it." She turns around and glares at me as if this is hitting close to home. "I won't be confined to this mansion any longer because you're scared someone is going to try and kill me."

Violet's feistiness is a quality I admire about her, but right now, it's just irritating. Until I remove the threat to her life, she has to live within the confines of my home.

"You will not be leaving this house. I am going to get rid of the threat, but until then, you stay inside. Do you understand me?"

The rage in her crystal blue eyes is blazing brightly. "Why don't you marry this woman your father arranged for you? That way I'm off the hook from being murdered, and you don't have to worry about having anyone to lose," she says, tears welling up in her eyes.

I know she doesn't mean it, but she has a point. If I wanted to save Violet's life, all I'd have to do is tell Duarte I will marry his whore of a daughter. "That's not what I meant, Vi. Why are you taking this the wrong way?" I step toward her, but she takes a step backward. "I won't marry her because I-I…" It's almost impossible to speak those three words I know she wants me to utter. It's as if my brain is hard-wired not to let them past my lips.

"You what, Dante?" Violet stares at me impatiently.

I shake my head. "I want to marry you."

She looks wounded that I still can't tell her how I feel. I watch after her as she spins around and heads back toward her room.

"Where are you going?" I call after her.

"Away from you," she replies.

She walks right out of the door into the corridor in her nightdress and thin robe.

"Vi, stop." She breaks into a run, dashing away from me. "Fuck's sake." I walk after her calmly as I won't run after her in my own home. "Where the fuck are you going?" I call after her.

Initially, I think she's playing a game and wants me to chase after her through my house like an idiot. Then, I realize where she is heading. I quicken my pace, hoping I won't be too late. She's trying to head for the front door and out of my home. It's not safe for her, especially after the call I just received.

I can't lose Violet. She's the only person I've ever loved, and I won't have her ripped from me so easily. Even if I can't tell her yet how much she means to me, she will come to learn the truth eventually. We are made for each other. I want her to be my wife because I love her, but I don't know why I can't tell her that.

21

VIOLET

*M*y heart is pounding as I try to run away from the man who I professed my love to only last night. He can't say it back, which means either he doesn't love me, or he can't open up to me. Whichever of those it is, I can't risk more heartache from him.

All of this bullshit because he's too scared that he's going to lose me. I've lost people in my life who weren't involved in criminal organizations. Death is a part of life, and if he isn't willing to face that truth for me, he can't love me the way I love him—with all of my heart.

Initially, I hated him for snatching away my free will and for the things he is capable of doing to other human beings. Killing is never okay, and I'm still unsure how I could ever be with him and accept that as a part of his life.

The hate didn't hold long, as my love for him existed before I knew every dark secret about his life. A love too strong to be broken by the darkness he holds inside of him. Even so, it's not a love I can nurture any longer, not unless I want to end up hurt beyond repair.

I rush out of the front door of Dante's home and onto the driveway at the front. I don't have a plan other than getting the fuck away from him fast. I run to the left, knowing that I've got no chance of heading out the main entrance.

Quickly, I glance over my shoulder to be sure Dante didn't follow me. When I look in front of me again, I collide with a man. A man I don't recognize is smirking down at me. "Exactly who I was looking for," he says.

"Who are you?"

His smirk is almost evil as he grabs hold of me forcefully. "Never mind that, señorita. Why are you outside the safety of Dante's mansion?"

I swallow hard, realizing Dante was right. The moment I stepped out of his home I ran right into the arms of his enemy.

"Let go of me," I say, trying to twist away from his grasp.

The man tightens his hold on my arms and pulls me closer. "There's no use trying to fight." He's so strong I can't break free.

Panic claws at my heart as he brings a cloth up to my face. I look away, trying desperately not to inhale whatever the cloth is doused in. It's no use as his strength overpowers all of my attempts.

"Violet. Where are you?" Dante calls out of the front door, but I'm hidden behind trees to the left of his home.

Fuck.

I can't respond to his calls and let him know I'm in danger. It drives home how out of depth I am in this situation. Dante tried to explain that staying in his home was a safety measure until he could deal with the problem. I'm a fucking idiot for not listening to him.

I try to make a noise behind the cloth he holds against my mouth, but slowly I feel the effects of whatever drug he used on the cloth clouding my mind. It won't be long until I'm out cold.

"Vi?" Dante calls my name again, closer this time.

A glimmer of hope ignites inside of me, knowing that I'll be out cold before too long. The man holding me tightens his grip and slowly moves away, dragging me along the ground.

I fumble with the clasp of my mother's bracelet around my wrist, hoping I can free it. A clue for Dante to find. It doesn't mean he will know I've been taken for sure, but he might. It's my only chance. Dante is my only chance.

My eyes shut as the metal clinks softly onto the ground. The man is too focused on Dante to notice as he continues to move us further from the house. All I see behind my shut eyelids is Dante's beautiful face as he smiles that rare but warm smile at me.

Every Friday night, he always smiled at me like that, but I've hardly seen it since he kidnapped me. Dante, the guitarist of a band, and Dante, the powerful drug cartel leader, are worlds apart. It's as though he has split personalities.

The man who attacked me hauls me over his shoulder forcefully before stuffing me into the trunk of a car. The slam of it shutting makes me jump.

After that, everything goes blank, and I know without a doubt that my life is over before it truly began.

WHEN I WAKE, I'm sitting in a dark office, bound to a chair. A foul-tasting piece of cloth is forced into my mouth and tightly tied at the back of my head.

I groan at the pain tearing through my head as the drugs I'd been knocked out with are still affecting me. My vision is blurry as I try to move. The bindings around my body are so tight I can't move at all.

It's been quite a few years since I've felt this vulnerable and helpless. Ever since I escaped my stepdad's clutches, I've done everything for myself. In life, you can only rely on yourself. It angers me that Dante has snatched that freedom away from me, like he snatched my whole life from me.

I should hate him with a passion after everything he's put me through. Instead, I love him as much as ever. I would have run away if he could tell me he loved me back.

"Look who is awake," A voice says from behind me.

I hate that I can't turn around or fight at all. "Who are you?" I demand, making sure to infuse as much confidence in my tone as possible, even though inside I'm a mess.

He chuckles softly. "It doesn't matter who I am. It matters who you are to Dante Ortega."

I swallow hard. "I'm no one but a slave to him."

"Bullshit," he spits, walking in front of me. "You are his fiancé, chica. It makes you valuable." The guy has jet black hair slicked over his head with way too much hair product and graying teeth. He's a smoker, and one of his teeth at the front has been replaced with a gold one.

I shake my head. "That's not true. I signed a contract to be his fiancé for two months on a trial basis. I'm nothing more than a business arrangement."

That gets his interest as he raises a brow. "A contract, huh?" He steps closer to me and grips my chin between his finger and thumb, forcing me to look up at him. "So, you're a whore, then?"

I grit my teeth. "No. I'm not a whore, I'm a bartender." I try not to let his degrading comment get under my skin, but I can't help it. Guys like this are everything that's wrong with the world.

"How long was I knocked out?" I ask, trying to look for a window to gauge whether it's still day or night.

He chuckles and walks around me in a circle. "You don't get to ask the questions here."

I narrow my eyes at him as he returns to stand in front of me. "What are you going to do with me?"

There's a sick amusement dancing in his almost jet-black eyes. He licks his lip in a way that makes my stomach churn, and I know I'm not going to like his answer. "I want to find out why Dante was so desperate to fuck you that he made you sign a contract." He rubs his hand across the front of his pants, and dread sinks my stomach like a lead weight.

"Don't you fucking think about it," I say.

He growls and brings the back of his hand down hard

across my face. "You don't speak to me like that, chica. Do you understand?"

I glare at him, despite the sting across my cheek. There's no way I'm doing anything with this guy. If he puts his cock in my mouth, I'll bite the damn thing off. The thought of any man other than Dante touching me makes me want to throw up.

"Open that dirty mouth of yours, whore," he orders, unbuttoning his jeans.

I shake my head. "No chance. If you put anything in my mouth, I'll bite." I hold his gaze to make sure he's aware that I'm deadly serious.

He laughs and walks away from me. I wonder if perhaps he's thought against putting anything in my mouth. Instead, he returns with some gadget that makes my stomach sink. "I'd like to see you try when this gag is fitted." He proceeds to fit the straps to my face while I try and fail to fight him.

"Your disgusting," I spit, struggling to speak with this stupid open mouth gag in my mouth.

He smirks at me. "I'm going to enjoy working out exactly why Dante is so taken with you." He finishes fastening it. "I wonder if you've got a magic mouth or cunt. Only one way to find out."

I try to pull my arms out of the bindings, but it's no use. My captor disappears, and I hear him rummaging around behind me. He grunts, and I look over my shoulder to see him with his flaccid penis out, trying to get it hard.

My stomach twists, and I think I'm about to puke. I train my eyes forward and do something I haven't done in a long time. I start to pray that I can be saved from this man—from this fate. I can't undo all the bad shit I've done in my life, but suddenly on the cusp of being thrown back into that position of abuse from a weak and pathetic man, I can't help myself.

It's all I can do. As I keep my eyes clamped shut, Dante's face appears in my mind. God can't help me now, not since I've been to bed with the Devil. My fate rests in his hands.

Will he save me?

22

DANTE

I hold the silver bracelet that Violet always wore in my hands, feeling the weight of her loss ready to crush me at any moment.

"Boss, what do you want us to do?" Alejandro, my head of security, asks.

I shake my head. "Is there no way of identifying the man from the CCTV?" I ask.

Having found no trace of Violet on the property after searching every square mile, they found footage of a man taking my woman.

Alejandro clicks his fingers at one of his security guards. The man comes forward with the footage from the CCTV. "We were unable to get a match when we ran it through the police database." Alejandro shakes his head. "Maybe you'll recognize the man, sir?"

He passes me the video, but it is grainy as hell. I feel rage infecting my blood at the sight of another man's hands on my princess. There's no way anyone could identify this man from the photos.

"Have we heard anything back on getting clearance for the CCTV footage for the roads nearby?" Knowing our only chance of finding a culprit is to rely on finding a vehicle and possible suspect in the vicinity of my home at that time.

Alejandro shakes his head. "Not yet, but Detective Hernandez is working on it as we speak."

I nod. "Good. I want every one of our men out on the street, searching for answers." I slam my hands down on the desk. "This is an attack on the cartel. No one takes what is mine," I growl.

Alejandro's eyes widen slightly, as he hasn't seen me lose my shit before. I can't help it. Violet is everything to me.

"That will be all, Alejandro." I wave my hand toward the door to dismiss him. My men can't be around me when I'm like this. It brings in to question my feelings for the woman who was taken.

He bows his head and turns, signaling for Daniel to leave ahead of him. I watch as they disappear out of my office, gently shutting the door behind them. I stand and pace the floor of my office, feeling out of control. There hasn't been a time in my life I've felt so panicked about anything.

I walk to my dresser and pour myself a glass of whiskey since I've run out of rum. I knock back the entire glass and go to pour myself another when my phone rings.

I dig it out of my pocket. "Father," I answer.

"Son, Duarte hired Felipe Ortiz to kidnap your woman."

There's a stern sound in his voice as he bluntly relays the information to me.

I clench my jaw as Felipe Ortiz is hired muscle, but the worst kind. He only preys on women and the elderly, people who can't put up a fight. Thankfulness spreads through me that Gerado was stupid enough to hire a Mexican to carry out his dirty work in New York City. There's no Mexican who operates underground that I don't know inside out. Ortiz operates from an old, rundown industrial park on the other side of Queens.

"Thank you, father. I can handle that piece of shit easily."

"Son." My father rarely calls me that. "I will deal with Duarte for you here. He has disrespected our cartel, and for that, he will pay." There's a moment's pause. "You may have broken an engagement, but you have the right to do that as the heir to our operations."

"Thank you, that means a lot. I thought you disapproved of my choice to marry an American."

More silence follows. "I'm proud that you are becoming your own man and sticking up for what you want, no matter the cost." With that, he cancels the call.

As I stare at the wall, my chest aches, wondering if I heard my father tell me he was proud of me. It shouldn't mean so much, not from a man who ripped so much from me as a child. My mother for one and then my sister. He has done so much bad in my life, and I would never go so far as to say I love him, but I can't help but crave his approval even after everything.

Javier enters the room without knocking. "Jefe, the CCTV

footage from nearby roads has come through, but we can't identify the guy who took her. At least no cars that are on our radar flagged up. It will take a while for us to sift through and cross-reference plates with possible suspects."

I shake my head and turn to face him. "No need. My father called, and Duarte employed Felipe Ortiz."

Javier raises a brow. "Seriously?"

I nod. "Yeah, what an amateur."

"Let's go and pay that son of a bitch a visit then," Javier says, rubbing his hands together.

None of us ever liked Felipe, but this is the first time we've had a good reason to go after him. I'm surprised he had the balls to take a job against our operation.

I nod. "Grab some explosives from the armory and meet me out front."

Javier nods and goes to leave, but I grab his shoulder. "It will be just me and you. I don't trust anyone else to be involved in this rescue mission. Do you understand me?"

"Of course, jefe. My mouth will remain shut."

I'm thankful for Javier. We grew up together, and I know I can trust him with anything. My other men I trust, but not as much as him. Ric and Francisco are, of course, as trustworthy, but I don't need more than one of my men by my side to deal with this low life scum. The rescue will call my questionable feelings for Violet into question. I don't need word spreading that I'm going soft over a woman.

Javier rushes toward the armory to get the explosives. I grab the keys to my Ferrari off the console table. My friend has been dying to drive my Ferrari ever since I bought it a year ago. Today I'm going to give him that privilege.

I sit in the passenger's side of the car, waiting for him. When he comes out the door, he raises his brow, seeing me in the passenger's seat. "Come on, you're driving," I say out of the window to him.

He looks like a kid at Christmas as he chucks the bag of explosives in the small back seat and gets into the driver seat, turning over the engine. The purr of it beneath me is a satisfying sound, but I can hardly admire it right now. All I can think about is getting Violet back safely. "Drive like your life depends on it," I say.

Javier smiles, nodding. "You've got it, Jefe." He peels out of the driveway and onto the main road, heading speedily in the industrial estate direction.

It takes fifteen minutes to get to the shit tip Felipe Ortiz calls his business premises in average traffic. Anything under this would be good, but I know the longer she's in that degenerate's capture, the more damage he could do to her.

Ortiz only takes on women or older men. He hasn't got the balls to stand up to anyone of note. I'm surprised he is the best Duarte could get to do this job. "Can you believe Duarte left this kind of job to that waste of space?" I ask, glancing over at Javier, who is having too much fun behind the wheel of my car.

Javier shakes his head. "Not really. The guy could have enlisted someone with some balls." He sighs heavily. "Don't worry, sir. We're going to get your woman back in one piece." There's a look of determination in his eyes. "I won't have you feeling the pain of losing someone you love too. It can ruin you."

I clear my throat. "Who says I love her?"

Javier laughs. "I've known you've loved that señorita ever since you set eyes on her in that bar."

I run a hand across the back of my neck. "That obvious, huh?"

He shakes his head. "No, I've just known you a very long time, Dante. You've never looked at any woman the way you look at Violet."

I'm a fool not to have told her the truth. If I'd just told her those three words she so desperately craved, we wouldn't be in this mess. She ran out of that house because she believes I don't love her. It couldn't be further from the truth.

"You're right, but don't tell anyone else."

Javier smiles at me. "You don't even have to tell me, brother. I'll always have your back."

I nod, knowing that is true. Javier and I have been best friends since we were little, and that will never change. He's the keeper of all my secrets, and I'm the keeper of his.

"You know, it won't be easy to keep it a secret once you marry her, though, right?"

I shrug. "People need not know that it is anything but a marriage to further my bloodline. In public, we'll remain people joined only by the rings on our fingers. In private." I look at him and wink.

"It's not easy hiding from the world, but if you feel it best, then that's what you must do." He swallows hard. "I've been hiding far too long and always will."

I place my hand on his shoulder. "I'm sorry that you can't be yourself in our world. If I could change that, I would do in a heartbeat."

Javier nods. "I know, brother. Life sucks." He indicates and pulls into the industrial park where Ortiz has his office.

Javier parks the car in front of the building, and I feel the adrenaline pulsing through my veins increase.

Ortiz isn't stupid. He will have rigged the place. We will fight fire with fire. "The place will be rigged, that's what explosives are for." I grab the bag out from behind our seats. "Let's light the place up."

Javier's eyes flash with excitement as he unzips the bag and sets up the explosives on Felipe's industrial unit's door.

He walks back to join me, a safe distance from the door. "Ready, jefe?" he asks once he's finished setting up the detonator.

"Always."

Javier hits detonate, and the explosion blows the doors off and with it sets off another explosion from within, blowing any rigged traps he had set for intruders. It's time to make Felipe pay. After today, everyone will know that Violet is off-limits. I'll make an example out of this idiot if it's the last thing I do.

23

VIOLET

I can't believe this is happening. My nose crinkles as the pathetic excuse of a man strokes his little dick in his hand, inching closer to me. The guy is barely even hard. I try desperately to shut my mouth, but this damn contraption he has fitted makes it impossible.

Fuck.

I'm not often one to admit defeat too easily, but this is by far the most helpless I've ever felt in my life. There's nothing I can do to stop him. A roar of an engine breaks my stream of consciousness, and the guy's brow furrows as he glances toward the door.

He doesn't get distracted for long as he steps forward. "Time for me to test out your magic mouth, chica."

I shake my head. "You make me fucking sick," I spit, struggling to talk around this stupid gag keeping my mouth wide open.

He gets even closer, staring down at me with a sick and twisted look of pure delight in his eyes. This guy is fucking gross. His dick is now inches away from my mouth, and I can't watch.

I hear some commotion outside, followed by a huge explosion. The guy jumps away from me, startled. Thank god he didn't get the chance to shove his disgusting penis in my mouth.

Dante bursts through the door with wild rage consuming his dark eyes. "Get the fuck away from her," He roars, aiming his gun right at the man who kidnapped me and almost forced me to suck him off. The guy quickly shoves his flaccid penis back into his pants.

Relief washes over me. I would have been raped if Dante hadn't found me so quickly. I have no idea how he knew where I was, but I've never been more thankful to see anyone. Dante keeps the gun aimed at the man who kidnapped me.

My heart pounds frantically as I realize the danger of the situation. The guy has been caught off guard, but he will be armed. I watch Dante step closer to him and Javier, from the band, enters behind. He has his gun also drawn and aimed at my captor.

A flood of relief washes over me as I realize the asshole who stole me from Dante is outnumbered.

"Take a seat, Felipe. We need to have a chat," Dante says.

The man, who I guess is called Felipe, does as Dante says in a heartbeat. It's a surprise considering he was such an asshole to me. "Dante, I didn't realize the woman I'd been sent to kidnap was yours." He holds his hands up, which are shaking with fear. "Please, you have to believe me."

"Liar," I spit since he knew I was his fiancé. This gag makes it so damn difficult to speak.

Dante's rage consumed gaze meets mine, and he tilts his head to the side. "He knew you were my fiancé, didn't he?"

I nod in response, rather than trying to speak.

Javier steps behind Felipe, who is sitting down, and grabs hold of his wrists, binding them with rope.

Dante moves toward me while Javier is restraining the asshole that kidnapped me. "Are you okay?"

I nod in response as he unclips the gag that Felipe forced into my mouth to keep my jaw open. "I'm okay thanks to you." He frees me and then cuts the ropes around my body.

I can't help but jump up and wrap my arms tightly around his stomach. "You saved me just in time," I say, tears welling in my eyes.

All my life, I've relied on myself to get out of tricky situations. Dante's the first person to ever come to my rescue like that. I pull back from the embrace and move my hands behind his neck, pulling his lips to mine.

He kisses me desperately, holding my body flush against him. His tongue tangles with mine as our passion ignites instantly.

I cling to him with all my strength, knowing that after what just happened, I never want to be parted from him again.

Dante pulls away and stares down at me.

"I'm sorry about earlier," I say.

Dante shakes his head before pressing his forehead to

mine. "No, I'm the one who should be sorry." He brings my hand up to his mouth and kisses the back of it. "I love you, Violet."

My heart feels like it stops beating for a few beats as I stare into his dark, brown eyes. "Really?"

Dante nods. "I'm sorry I couldn't tell you earlier. I just… I've never said those words to anyone before in my life."

My throat closes up hearing him admit that to me. I'm the first person he's ever told he loves. My chest aches, and I feel the tears welling in my eyes again. They roll down my cheeks, but they are happy tears.

Dante wipes them away with his thumbs. "Don't cry, mi amor. Everything is going to be okay."

Javier clears his throat. "Hey, lovebirds. We've got an asshole to deal with if you forgot."

Dante looks over at Felipe, and the rage reignites in full force. He drops my hand, and his fists clench by his side. "I can't believe that asshole was going to stick his poor excuse of a dick in your mouth."

I can because he's a piece of shit. The kind of man that deserves to rot in hell.

Dante grabs hold of my shoulders firmly and looks me straight in the eye. "Please go outside and wait for me in the parking lot."

I feel reluctant about leaving him at all, and I don't particularly appreciate taking orders—unless it's in the bedroom. "No, I want to be here for this."

Dante growls softly. "No, princess. There is no way in hell you want to be here for this." He shakes me a little. "I can't have you witness what I have to do." He kisses my lips quickly. "Do as I say and wait for me outside, please."

"Okay, I'll wait outside." I nod in response as he has asked me nicely. I squeeze his hand one more time before heading toward the exit. My stomach twists as I walk past Felipe. There's a wet stain at his crotch where he's peed his pants, and he's shaking violently.

There is no doubt in my mind he will deserve everything Dante does to him, but I'm curious as to what he will do. As I slip out of the door and out of Dante's sight, I come to a halt. My curiosity over what exactly Dante is capable of forces me to stay where I am, considering returning to spy on him.

A deep, piercing scream echoes from the room, and my heart rate kicks up a few gears. I remain rooted to the spot, listening intently. If I'm going to marry Dante, I need to know what kind of a man he is. The good, the bad, and all the dark, twisted parts of him.

I quietly creep back toward the small office at the back of the warehouse, hearing another shrill shriek that could turn your blood to ice. For a moment, I consider turning back around and running the hell out of there.

Instead, I move the last three meters closer and peer through the crack in the door. The scene in front of me makes my stomach churn. Blood coats Dante's knuckles and drips to the floor, and he holds a sharp blade in his hands.

I can see Felipe sitting in the chair with a look of pure anguish on his face. Then, I see why. Dante has castrated him entirely, leaving nothing there. Blood gushes from him at a relenting speed. "No one touches my property, Felipe. You had this coming."

I turn away as my stomach churns, and I rush back toward the parking lot. My heart is pounding at a hundred miles an hour, and my brain doesn't know how to process what I saw. I plant my ass on the curb, staring mindlessly at the concrete of the parking lot.

Dante is more twisted than I ever could have imagined. I knew he'd hurt him and kill him. That was a given but chopping a man's dick and balls off is more extreme than anything that came to mind. I try to tell myself that he probably shoved that nasty penis into so many women's mouths and worse. He was a rapist and a predator.

The question is whether the man I've fallen in love with is any better. I hear another blood-curdling screech come from inside of the industrial unit, followed by the shot of a gun. My stomach sinks as I realize it's over.

Dante just killed a man, and I assume he will have that same cold stare as he had before when I saw him kill the first time. It's a part of him—ingrained so deeply inside of him I know it's something I either have to live with or not be with him. The latter thought fills me full of darkness and despair.

Javier is the first to exit the building, walking right past me and unlocking the Ferrari parked in front of the building. He peels away in the vehicle, and that's when I notice the town car parked on the other side of the parking lot.

Dante follows close behind. He's cleaned the blood from his hands, but it's splattered all over his shirt. A reminder of what he did. "Come on, princess. Let's go home." He holds his hand out to me, and I hesitate a moment.

I put my hand in his, and he pulls me to my feet, leading me toward the town car. The man driving it nods at Dante as we get in the back. Dante sits close to me, placing his hand on my thigh. Although I know I want to marry this man, I can't help the thoughts that flood my mind.

If I agree to marry the devil, what does that make me?

24

DANTE

*V*iolet is quiet as I hold her against me in the back of the town car. Jorge had the respect to put up the privacy screen, but I'm not sure we needed it. She won't speak to me or look at me.

I shouldn't have allowed my brutality to spiral so far out of control with her nearby, but I couldn't help it. The man threatened my possession—Violet is mine. Something tells me that she didn't listen to me and wait outside the entire time.

When I joined her outside, she was as white as a sheet and wouldn't look me in the eye.

I remember her bracelet, which is in my jacket pocket. "You lost this, mi amor." I dig it out and hold it up to her.

She nods. "Yes, I unclipped it hoping you'd find it and know I'd been kidnapped." She swallows hard and looks at her hands in her lap.

I take her hand in mine and bring it to my lips. "You came back, didn't you?" I ask, holding her gaze intently.

Violet nods slowly. "I had to know what you are capable of, even though you told me to stay outside."

I tilt my head to the side slightly, knowing I'll have to punish her for disobeying me—something I will enjoy. "What did you see?"

She shuts her eyes briefly. "I saw you cut him his…" she shakes her head.

"You saw me castrate him?" I ask.

Violet swallows hard before nodding. "Yes."

"Don't you think that's what he deserved for what he would have undoubtedly done to you, princess?"

Vi meets my gaze and searches my eyes. I wonder what she is looking for, regret perhaps. An emotion she won't find from me. "How do you live with it?"

My brow furrows. "Live with what?"

"Live with doing such terrible things to people?"

I think about her question, knowing that the answer will never justify the crime in her mind. "It's who I am, mi amor. Felipe was a bad man, and he had raped countless women. I took justice into my own hands and made him pay for the wrong he has done because he crossed me." I shrug. "I'm a dark and twisted man, princess. Either you can live with that, or you can't."

She looks pensive, staring down at our entwined hands. I know how difficult it must be to hear that I have no reservations over what I did. I'd do it ten times over as well, and there's no use hiding that part of me from a woman I want to share my life with. If she does marry me, then I want our marriage to be open and truthful—the polar opposite of my parent's marriage.

"I think I can live with it," she says, looking up to meet my gaze. "I love you, Dante. All of you. Every twisted, dark part of you."

"Really?" I ask, searching her ice blue eyes for a hint of uncertainty. "You can love a man that has no qualms about cutting another man's manhood off or killing a man in cold blood?" It's almost impossible to believe that a woman so sweet and innocent can accept that part of me. "You can accept all of that and live with it without trying to change me?"

She nods slowly. "Yes, it's a lot, and I'm not saying I agree with what you do." She stares blankly at me. "All I'm saying is that life is so much better when you're in it. I'll live with anything if it means I can have you by my side."

I kiss her passionately. Even after everything she has seen me do and everything I've put her through, she still loves me. It's hard to believe I'm that lucky to find a woman so open to my dark and twisted side. "So, you will marry me?" I ask when I break free.

She smiles her beautiful, alluring smile. "I will."

I kiss her again, making her moan into my mouth as my tongue plunders hers with a renewed intensity. When we break apart, she is breathless. "Might want to slow it down until we get back."

I raise a brow. "The privacy screen is up."

She shoots me an irritated glare. "Dante. No."

"Wrong answer, princess." I kiss her neck, making her

moan loudly. "You know I hate being told no." I slip my hand up her nightgown and rub her clit roughly.

She hisses in pleasure, grabbing hold of the door pull. I kiss her lips, savoring the taste of her. I know I'll never get enough of my princess. I remove my fingers from her suddenly, and she watches me curiously.

Slowly, I place them in my mouth and suck the juices from them.

She moans as her pupils dilate even more. "Dante," she murmurs my name.

"That'll be all until we get home," I say, patting her thigh gently.

She groans in frustration. "That's not fair. You can't stop what you started."

I kiss her lips softly. "Remember how good it feels when I delay your gratification."

She doesn't look pleased with me but doesn't complain as she knows how good it is when I delay her orgasm. The ride back to the house feels like it drags, but I know that's because I can't wait to make love to my fiancé. She's my fiancé now because she wants to marry me, not because of some stupid contract I made her sign.

When we get back, I open the car door and help her out. Jorge drives away, leaving us alone in front of my house. "I'm so glad I got to you when I did, princess." I cup her chin in my hands and kiss her softly.

She nods. "Me too. I didn't want to suck that disgusting man's dick."

I growl in anger at the mere thought of him putting

his dick anywhere near her. How close he was to her was too fucking close. "Come on. I'm going to fuck you senseless." I lift her and put her over my shoulder. "Time to make you forget all other cocks for the rest of your life."

Violet laughs. "I think you've already achieved that, Dante."

"There's no harm in making certain." I carry her to my room—our room now. Once inside, I place her gently down onto the bed. "Strip," I order.

Her eyes dilate with a sensual thirst that drives me insane. She slowly pulls her sexy black slip off and reveals her lacy bra and matching panties. As she reaches for the waistband of her panties, I stop her. "Wait."

She tilts her head to the side slightly, giving me a questioning look.

"I want to show you something," I explain.

"Show me what?"

I hold up a hand and grab the blindfold on my nightstand. "It's a secret." I fasten the blindfold over her eyes before wrapping a gown around her. "Come on." If she will be my wife, she needs to understand how my tastes are more extreme than anything we've done yet.

We walk down the corridor, and I punch in my code on the keypad to open the door to my sex room.

I walk Violet inside and shut the door behind us. "Are you ready to learn how kinky your husband to be is?" I breathe into her ear, pulling the gown away from her.

"Yes," she breathes. The uncertainty in her voice makes

me harder than nails. She's a little scared, and that turns me on more than it should.

"Good girl." I undo the blindfold behind her head and reveal the room.

She gasps at the sight of all the whips, chains, cages, swings, horses and benches crowding the room in front of her. "What the…" She shakes her head. "What is this place?"

"My sex room or dungeon, whatever you want to call it." I walk further into the room, running my hand over the sex bench that I've wanted to bend her over since she got here. "I'm a Dom, after all, princess. I love it when you submit to me, and instruments make it more fun."

She walks into the room, looking at all the things I have in here. In particular, she seems interested in the swing. "That's for having sex on?"

I nod. "Yeah, do you want to try it now?"

Her eyes widen. "I've got no idea."

"We don't have to do anything in here now if you don't want." I move toward her and set my hands on her shoulders. "I just want you to know everything about me."

She smiles weakly at me. "I want to try, Dante." She shakes her head. "I don't know where to start."

I laugh at that. "How about with this?" I ask, walking to the bench I had in mind. It will keep her spread out wide, giving me access to every inch of her body.

She walks over and runs a hand over it. "We can try it." The uncertainty in her voice only makes me want to fuck her more. I know how sick that is.

"What we've tried up to now is the tip of the iceberg,

princess." I grab a Shibari rope off the rack and unravel it. "Strip for me."

Her smooth, creamy throat bobs as she swallows before unwrapping the gown from her body. I step toward her, my eyes roaming every inch of her perfect body. I kiss her neck and then whisper in her ear, "Since I'm taking it up a notch, we should have a safe word."

She raises a brow. "A safe word?"

I nod and wrap an arm around her neck, pulling her back into me. "Yes, a word you say if it gets too much for you and you need me to stop."

"What about stop?" she asks.

I laugh. "That's not very inventive, is it?"

She shrugs. "What do you suggest then?"

"How about purple?" I ask.

Violet smiles. "Like my name is a shade of purple." She nods. "I like it."

"That's settled then." I start to tie my Shibari rope around her breasts and waist, ensuring all the pressure points are right. "Bondage can be stimulating if you know what you are doing, princess," I breathe, feeling my cock throbbing against my tight boxer briefs as I work on the knots. "And, lucky for you, I know what I'm doing."

She's trembling when I finish, eyes wide as she looks down at the rope snaking around her waist and breasts. I've not seen anything more alluring than the way she looks right now.

"Now, be a good girl and get on the bench." I pat it.

She walks over to it but struggles to climb on with the bindings. I help her, forcing her legs onto the leg rests, which keep her thighs spread wide apart. I strap her ankles in first with the fitted restraints, then her wrists at the front. It's a sight I'm going to memorize forever as her spread pussy drips onto the leather beneath her.

I slap her ass softly with my palm, and she jerks instinctively. "I want to fuck your pussy." I rub my finger through her soaking wet lips and then move past it to her tempting ass hole. "And then your ass, princess." I apply pressure on her tight, little hole. "Have you ever been fucked in the ass before?"

Violet shakes her head. "No."

I groan at the thought of being the first man to give her that pleasure. "Do you want daddy to fuck your ass?"

There are a few moments of silence. "I'm not sure."

I spank her ass cheek hard. "You'll be sure by the time I'm ready to enter your tight little hole and pop your anal cherry."

She visibly shudders, making excitement rise inside of me.

I strip out of my clothes and then grab a lube bottle and vibrator off a dresser.

She's practically gushing from her pussy when I return, anticipating what I'm going do to her tight ass. It makes me feel more powerful than anything else in this world—the way I affect her.

I squirt lube onto her tight ring of muscles before gently pressing my finger through it.

She gasps, tensing the moment I slip inside her untouched cavity. "Dante, I'm not sure—"

I turn on the vibrator I grabbed from the counter and press it firmly against her clit. Her whole body jolts from the force, and she comes undone almost at once.

"Oh fuck, yes, daddy, yes," she screams.

I start to fuck my finger in and out her tight hole, loosening it with every plunge. Once I'm sure she can handle another, I add a second, third and then fourth until she's practically gaping.

Her moans are like music to my ears as I keep edging her clit with the wand and finger fucking her in the ass. "You are daddy's dirty little whore, aren't you?" I ask.

She nods her head frantically. "Yes, fuck, yes," she pants.

I can't help but smile at the way I always turn her into such a needy little girl. "Do you want daddy's cock in that tight virgin ass?"

She tenses slightly but nods. "Yes, daddy."

I fist my throbbing, aching cock in my hands and position it at the entrance of her pussy. "First, I want to feel that tight little pussy come for me. Then, I'm going to take your anal virginity, princess."

She moans loud as I rub the tip of my cock through her dripping pussy, before plowing every inch deep inside her. I thrust three fingers into her ass at the same time, making her feel the sensation of something in her ass and pussy all at once. The thought of fucking her ass while her pussy is stuffed full with a huge dildo makes me groan, but baby steps first.

"It feels so… Oh, fuck, yes," she cries, sounding over-whelmed by the sensation.

I pull my fingers out of her ass and start to pound into her harder, grabbing her hips forcefully and roughly taking her. I grab a fistful of her hair and pull her toward me. "I bet you can't wait for my cock to stretch that tight little ass out for real, can you?"

She moans, eyes rolling back in her head. "I can't wait, daddy. Oh fuck, I'm coming," she screams as she tumbles over the edge, her perfect pussy clamping down around my thick cock hard.

I spank her ass. "Daddy didn't tell you to come yet, princess."

"Sorry," she pants as I let go of her hair.

"Time for me to fuck that ass real good," I growl, fisting my cock in my hand and staring at it. The hunger I feel to take Violet in the ass controls me.

I squirt lube all over my cock, getting it ready. I rub the tip of my cock over her hole a few times before positioning it just right and pressing inside.

"Fuck, that hurts," she screams as I relentlessly push through her tight ring of muscles.

"Relax, princess. It won't hurt soon." I continue to push until half my cock is buried inside her ass and then give her a moment to get used to the sensation. She's tighter than I imagined.

Violet trembles. "It fucking hurts."

I spank her ass. "Give it a chance." I start to move out of her, and she groans.

"It feels odd."

I spank her ass again. "Don't make me gag you, Vi."

She turns silent and allows me to stretch out her hole, slowly pushing a little further with each thrust. Before long, she's moaning and panting beneath me as the tempo increases.

"That's it, baby, take daddy's cock in your ass," I growl, as I feel my control slipping.

"Oh god, yes," she shouts as I grab hold of one of the ropes around her waist and start to pull her back into me hard. I watch as my too thick cock pulls at the muscles of her tight asshole with each thrust. It's almost impossible to stop myself from coming as she's so fucking tight.

"I want you to come for me, princess. I want you to come with my cock buried in your ass."

Violet moans louder as I fuck her harder. I know I won't be able to last much longer, but I have to. Until she comes, I will keep fucking her like the beast I am.

"I'm close, daddy," she cries.

I reach my fingers around and shove two in her pussy, curling them to hit the spot inside of her. It's all it takes to send her over the edge.

Violet comes undone, screaming daddy over and over again like a broken record. I unleash my seed deep in her ass, marking her as mine entirely.

Every inch of her I own now, forever.

EPILOGUE

VIOLET

*O*ne year later...

The villa on the Gulf of Mexico is stunning, but I struggle to enjoy the beauty. I'm going to meet Dante's father for the first time today, and from everything he has told me, I'm not looking forward to it at all.

It's odd that we've been together and year, and I'm three months pregnant, and only now I'm meeting his family. Our wedding is tomorrow, and we are meeting his father for dinner, which is in less than an hour. Pedro patrols the beach in front of the house, and he catches my gaze, waving swiftly at me.

I smile and wave back.

Dante doesn't approve of my friendship with my body-guard, so much so he tried to get me a new one. I put my foot down and insisted that I either have Pedro or no one.

"Bonita," Dante says, stepping out onto the balcony behind me.

I smile at him. "Hey."

He walks toward me and wraps his arms around my waist, kissing my neck. "How are you feeling?"

I draw in a deep breath. "Nervous as hell."

Dante spins me around to face him, pressing me against the metal railings of the balcony. "You shouldn't be nervous, princess. My father will be happy to hear our news."

I swallow hard. "The stories you've told me about your father suggest otherwise."

Dante shakes his head. "No, my father may be a heartless bastard, but he wants an heir to the empire." He kisses me softly. "Another Ortega to take over the operations once both of us are gone."

My conflict over that is one I struggle to even contend with. Dante insists there's no other choice for our firstborn son. He will be next in line to inherit the dark and twisted job as head of a Mexican drug cartel.

"And, if it's a girl?" I ask.

He tilts his head to the side slightly. "If it's a girl, we keep going until we have a boy."

I swallow hard, wondering if Dante would ever be as heartless as his father was to his sister when it comes to our daughter if we have one. "Something has been on my mind ever since you told me what happened to your sister."

His brow furrows. "What is it, mi amor?"

I press my hands against his chest to free myself and pace the length of the balcony. "Would you ever be so heartless to our daughter if we ever have a girl?"

The look of pure disappointment enters his beautiful, dark

brown eyes. "You believe me capable of something that terrible to my flesh and blood?"

I shake my head, knowing deep down I don't believe he would do something so cruel to me. I will love our children with all my heart, and if he were to take any of them from me, I could never forgive him. "No, but I just…" I trail off, knowing that my concern over Dante one day becoming his father is irrational.

Dante walks toward me and gently cups my face in his hands. "I'm not my father, Vi. It hurts me that you think I could ever be that cruel. I will love every one of our children equally, no matter their gender." The sincerity in his tone cuts me to the core, and I know how stupid it was for me to think otherwise. "I'm a brutal man, and that's something I'll never apologize for. It's part of me, but you can only ever expect love from me to you and our children."

I swallow hard, knowing that I've witnessed how brutal he can be with men who cross him. Even so, I know that Dante will be an amazing father, even if our world isn't the ideal place for children. He will protect them with everything he's got. "I'm sorry. I'm just scared of meeting a man who can be so evil."

He nods. "I understand." He entwines our hands together. "Believe me. I would never have brought you here if I thought he posed any threat to you, princess." He kisses me again. "Or our baby, whether it be a boy or a girl." He pulls away and checks his watch. "We better get going if we are going to be on time to meet my father for dinner. He hates tardiness."

I don't want to make a bad impression on his father. He

takes my hand and leads me toward the grand hallway. If I thought Dante's place was extravagant, it's nothing compared to this home.

A dark-haired man with peppered gray running through it stands in the center of the hallway. He turns at the sound of us descending the stairs. There's no doubt that he's Dante's father. He's an older version of him, but they look so alike. "Bienvenido mi hijo,"

"Thank you, father." Dante slips his hand lower on my back. "I want you to meet my fiancé, Violet McKenzie."

He has a cold expression as he nods his head. "It's good to meet you, Miss. Kenzie."

I swallow hard. "And you, Mr. Ortega. Please call me Violet."

He nods and then moves his gaze to his son. "Shall we?"

"Sure. Is Elena joining us tonight?" He asks.

His father's eyes narrow. "Elena passed away." There's a coldness in his tone—a coldness that sends shivers down my spine.

I don't know who Elena was, but something tells me that his father probably had a hand in her demise.

"Sorry to hear that," Dante says, seemingly unfazed by his father's declaration.

A young woman who has to be even younger than me comes down the stairs in a stunning white dress. She walks over to Raúl and kisses him passionately in front of us.

My eyes widen, since Raúl is more than old enough to be her father—maybe even her grandfather, but hey who am I to judge? She's beautiful, that's for sure.

"Dante, Violet, meet Cindy, my fiancé."

Dante takes her hand and kisses the back of it. "Lovely to meet you."

I give her a warm smile. "It's lovely to finally meet Dante's family," I say.

His father gives me a cautious glance and then looks away. "Follow me to the dining room."

Dante keeps his hand firmly on the small of my back as he guides me after his father. I can't deny that I'm nervous, and my first conversation with Raúl Ortega is not helping ease my anxiety. He's cold and unreadable, exactly as I expected him to be.

We sit in a grand dining hall quite far from Raúl, who sits at the head of the table. "Please eat," he orders.

An uncomfortable silence settles around the room as the four of us start to eat. Dante is the first to break that silence. "So, how long have you and Cindy been engaged?"

Cindy smiles and gazes adoringly at Raúl, who hardly even looks at her. "It's six months next week. We're so excited to plan the wedding."

Raúl clears his throat. "Correction. You're so excited."

She sets her hand on his wrist gently and laughs. "Surely you're looking forward to marrying me, my love."

He shrugs nonchalantly and glances right at me with his ice-cold stare. "Are you excited to marry my son?"

I swallow hard, feeling like I'm being put on trial. One wrong answer and I could be put on death row, literally. "Very much. I'm excited to start a family with him." I meet Dante's gaze, and he smiles, squeezing my hand under the table.

"Indeed. We have some news to that effect. Violet is three months pregnant with our first child."

For the first time since we met, I see a whisper of a smile on Raúl's lips. "Wonderful news. A wife must be able to produce an heir, and it looks like you aren't wasting any time." He claps his hands. "A toast to the Ortega family line getting stronger with this union." He lifts his glass of wine, and we all lift ours too, mine filled with water since I'm pregnant. "I was unsure about an American woman polluting our bloodline, but perhaps this is what the cartel needed. A new direction for a modern era."

Everyone says cheers in a chorus, including me, reluctantly since it was a shit toast if you ask me.

Polluting the bloodline? What is he, royalty?

I keep my thoughts to myself and continue to eat my food reservedly.

Raúl speaks again. "I thought as you don't have a father, Violet, that I could walk you down the aisle tomorrow. If you would like."

I'm not sure what is worse, walking down the aisle with a man so cold and calculating as Raúl Ortega, or walking down it alone. "It would be an honor, Mr. Ortega."

He shakes his head. "Please, call me Raúl. That's settled then. I'm looking forward to the wedding."

Surprisingly, the atmosphere from that moment on eases a little, and we have a relatively uneventful dinner talking about everyday things any normal family might talk about.

My reservations about meeting the ruthless and powerful drug lord were unfounded, thankfully. All I hope is that tomorrow goes by without a hitch. Life is unpredictable when you are engaged to a man like Dante.

THE SUN IS STARTING to set in the sky, casting the most beautiful orange hue across the wedding arch and chairs set up on the beach.

My stomach is a bundle of nerves as I take Dante's father's arm. He gives me a smile, which isn't altogether kind. I knew that his offer to walk me down the aisle wasn't an offer but an order. Even so, it beats walking down it alone.

"Ready?" he asks.

I nod. "As ready as I'll ever be, sir," I add the sir, as after our dinner last night, it's clear he expects respect from everyone.

He smiles and gives the nod to the officiant, who starts the music. My heart is pounding frantically in my chest as we start down the long white isle set out over the soft sand.

Dante is standing in a breathtaking cream suit with a white shirt unbuttoned. The tattoo on his chest is just visible, along with the dark, short hair over his chest, and he looks devastatingly beautiful in the orange hue of the sunset.

He smiles his stunning smile at me as I start to walk toward him. The band plays the wedding march, and I do march, increasing my pace with each step.

Any anxiety over going through with this vanishes once he's in my sights. My baby's father is my soul mate, and I have no reservations about marrying him—not anymore.

Dante is ruthless and brutal, but I know he will protect our children and me with everything he's got. This life isn't what I envisaged for myself, but it's far more rewarding than any life I could have imagined.

Once I get to the end of the aisle, the officiant asks who gives me away. It feels a little odd, as Dante's father says he does. Something tells me if he didn't like me, pregnant or not, he would have got rid of me some way. He does indeed hold power, and by giving me away, it shows his blessing for our union.

The ceremony passes by in a blissful blur as we say our vows, staring into each other's eyes as if we are the only two people on the planet. For that time during the ceremony, that's exactly how it feels. Until the cheers erupt from our guests, basically only people that Dante knows because I wasn't allowed to invite my friends.

He made an exception for Alice, who has been my best friend ever since I arrived in New York City to be my maid of honor and only bridesmaid. She doesn't know the full story and never will, but I've been allowed to maintain our friendship, which means everything to me.

The reception marquee is set up a little way down the beach, and the music is already playing. I can smell the delightful scent of seafood and Mexican spices coming from there as we make our way to the party. Dante's hand remains tight around mine. All I want to do is spend the rest of the night tangled up in bed with my husband. Although, I know it's far too early for us to disappear from our wedding yet.

We walk into the marquee, which is beautifully laid out

with long white tables and elegant china. It's like something out of a fairytale, with huge chandeliers hanging down from the structure. "Wow, it's beautiful," I murmur.

Dante pulls me into his chest. "Not half as beautiful as you, princess."

I smile at my husband, feeling overwhelmed by the happiness inside of me. "You know what is on my mind right now?"

He leans in closer to me, teasing his lips over the lobe of my ear. "Daddy's cock?"

I draw in a sharp breath, feeling the desire flooding between my thighs. "Yes," I reply.

He groans softly. "How about I take you outside and have my way with you?"

I pull back and meet his gaze. "We can't disappear this early in the night."

Dante smirks at me, and I know it's a bad idea to suggest we can't do anything to him. It only makes him more determined to do it. "Is that right, princess? I'll prove you wrong about that." He drags me back out of the marquee and a short distance away toward his father's house. The swimming pool is lit up, and there's a wall where the showers are built in. "Perfect," he says.

I glare at him. "You think this is the perfect place for us to consummate our marriage?"

He nods. "I'm going to make you scream so loud they'll hear you in the reception." He wraps his arms around my waist and lifts me, moving toward the wall.

I gasp as my back collides with the rough, cold concrete. "Dante, what about my dress?"

He shrugs. "I'll be gentle."

I laugh at that. "You don't know the meaning of the word."

He plants kisses against my collarbone before biting hard enough to hurt. "You're right. Fuck the dress. I'll tear it off you if I want," he growls before covering my lips with his mouth. The ferocity in his kiss drives me wild. His hard, muscled body pins me against the wall as I keep my arms around his neck and my legs around his hips.

Dante let's go of me, forcing me to hold myself up with all my strength. He pulls down the straps on my dress and reveals my breasts to his hungry gaze, groaning as he sucks on each of my nipples. Then, he frees his thick, hard cock from the confines of his cream suit pants.

I moan at the sight of his cock standing upright and ready to take me against this wall like a wild beast.

"Tell me how much you want daddy's cock, princess," he orders, biting my shoulder.

I feel the need tighten inside of me. "I want it more than anything, daddy," I say, feeling so desperate to have every inch of him stretching me.

Dante sucks on my nipples one by one, driving me wild. I know he's not going to give me what I want without teasing me. "Please, daddy, fuck me."

He bites my bottom lip between his teeth so hard I think it might bleed. "I can't wait to make you my wife officially," he growls before using his free hand to tear my panties in two.

I feel his fingers delve inside of me as he groans. "Always so fucking wet for me, aren't you, princess?"

I nod in response. "Yes, please give me your cock," I beg shamelessly.

Dante's hand rests on each of my asscheeks as he holds me up, spreading my pussy open. His cock nudges against my aching entrance. "Is this what you want, Mrs. Ortega?" he asks, holding my gaze with his dark, lust-filled eyes. "Your husband's hard cock claiming you out in the open against a wall for anyone to hear us on our wedding day?"

I can hardly take the anticipation anymore, feeling my juice dripping from me. "Yes, please, fuck me, daddy," I beg.

Dante growls like an animal and thrusts every inch of his cock deep inside of me roughly. It's all I need as every pleasure center in my body sets on fire. My head falls back against the wall, and I groan in satisfaction.

Dante doesn't give me a moment to adjust as he starts to fuck me without mercy. My back roughly grazes against the wall, but I don't care. All I care about is my husband's cock taking me and making me his.

"Fuck, you are so damn tight," he growls.

My nipples are hard, painful peaks, rubbing against the fabric of his shirt. "Oh god, yes," I cry as he continues to push me higher.

Dante shocks me by lifting me away from the wall and carrying me still impaled on his cock around to the pool area —an area lit up and very visible to prying eyes. He doesn't care. Instead, he lowers me down onto one of the pool beds and continues to fuck me roughly.

I run my hand down his muscled chest clad in a tight, white shirt, enjoying the feel beneath my hands.

Dante groans and grabs both my wrists in one hand, pinning them above my head. "No touching, princess."

I pout at him but can't help the excitement rising inside of me as his dominance comes to the surface.

"I'm in control. Do as your husband tells you." The order lights me on fire as I writhe beneath him, taking each hard thrust more willingly than the last.

"Fuck me harder," I moan.

Dante's dark brown eyes flash with the challenge, and he picks up the pace, taking me without mercy. I've unleashed the beast inside of him, and that's what I wanted.

He growls above me, fucking me so hard I wonder if I'll tear in two. "Take daddy's cock like a good girl, princess," he roars.

I feel myself getting close as my toes curl. "Yes, daddy, yes," I cry, not caring anymore who hears us or sees us—let them watch.

"That's it, princess. Come on your husband's cock," He orders, eyes wild with a passion that burns so hot it threatens to scold me. "I want to look into your eyes as you come for me."

"Fuck," I cry, feeling the walls of my pussy clamp down around his thick shaft. The intensity of my orgasm hits me in waves as our bodies and souls merge. I hold his gaze the entire time, watching the way he hungrily devours my orgasm, fucking me through every second of it.

He roars as he comes undone, holding my gaze as he does. "That's it, baby, milk daddy's cock," he grunts, pumping into me three more times before collapsing on top of me. His weight is crushing but feels good as his cock continues to throb deep inside of me.

"Fuck, that was——"

"Amazing," Dante finishes for me. He pulls out of me and rolls over, pulling my dress down to cover my pussy, which is dripping with his cum. "Come here, princess." He pulls me against his chest. "You're mine now, forever."

I smile up at him, feeling beyond satisfied. "I've been yours since the moment we met, and you know it."

"I do." He smirks. "But do you know that I've also been yours from the moment we met too?"

I raise a brow. "No. That's not true."

Dante nods and kisses the back of my hand. "I've loved you since I first set eyes on you, and that's the truth."

I sigh as he nibbles on the inside of my wrist softly, kissing up my arm. "If we're not careful, we'll never make it to our wedding reception."

"That is the plan, princess." He winks.

I shake my head. "You're impossible, and I love you for it."

He captures my lips hungrily as we stay under the stars, wrapped up in the warm cocoon of our love for each other.

THE END

THANK you for reading Her Cartel Daddy, the fourth & final book in The New York Mafia Doms series. I hope you enjoyed following Dante's & Violet's story.

My next book is part of a new series, the Boston Mafia Doms and it follows a rather vicious mafia leader, Milo Mazzeo and his arranged marriage to mafia princess Aida Altieri. This book will be available through Kindle Unlimited or to pre-order on Amazon.

Cruel Daddy: A Dark Mafia Arranged Marriage Romance

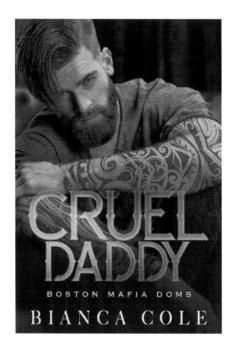

Cruelty is his middle name, and I'm at his mercy.

My father has kept me locked away in an ivory tower. I thought he wanted to protect me, but he only wanted to protect his asset. An untouched, sheltered mob princess is worth a lot of money to the right buyer.

My father's greed means Sicily is no longer big enough for him. I'm shipped across the Atlantic to Boston to marry a man I've never met, whose reputation for cruelty reaches as far as the shores of Sicily.

Milo Mazzeo is as dark as they come. He's a ruthless don with no morals, and he's about to become my husband. It's clear from the moment we meet that we have nothing in common.

Once we say I do, he tells me that I'm his possession. I must do whatever he says. I'm nothing more than a slave to tend to his every whim and need. If he thinks I'm going to accept my fate without a fight, he is mistaken.

I always expected to marry for love, but all I feel is hate toward this beautiful beast. They say there is a fine line between love and hate. Could the fire of hatred really twist into something more?

Cruel Daddy is the first book in the Boston Mafia Doms Series by Bianca Cole. This book is a safe story with no cliffhangers and a happily ever after ending. This story has some dark themes, hot scenes, and bad language. It features an over the top, twisted and possessive Italian crime boss.

ALSO BY BIANCA COLE

Wynton Series

Filthy Boss: A Forbidden Office Romance

Filthy Professor: A First Time Professor And Student Romance

Filthy Lawyer: A Forbidden Hate to Love Romance

Romano Mafia Brother's Series

Her Mafia Daddy: A Dark Daddy Romance

Her Mafia Boss: A Dark Romance

Her Mafia King: A Dark Romance

Bratva Brotherhood Series

Captured by the Bratva: A Dark Mafia Romance

Claimed by the Bratva: A Dark Mafia Romance

Bound by the Bratva: A Dark Mafia Romance

Taken by the Bratva: A Dark Mafia Romance

Royally Mated Series

Her Faerie King: A Faerie Royalty Paranormal Romance

Her Alpha King: A Royal Wolf Shifter Paranormal Romance

Her Dragon King: A Dragon Shifter Paranormal Romance

Her Vampire King: A Dark Vampire Romance

New York Mafia Doms Series

Her Irish Daddy: A Dark Mafia Romance

Her Russian Daddy: A Dark Mafia Romance

Her Italian Daddy: A Dark Mafia Romance

Her Cartel Daddy: A Dark Mafia Romance

Boston Mafia Doms Series

Cruel Daddy: A Dark Mafia Arranged Marriage Romance

ABOUT THE AUTHOR

Bianca Cole loves to write stories about over the top alpha bad boys who have heart beneath it all, fiery heroines, and happily-ever-after endings with heart. Her stories have twists and turns that will keep you flipping the pages, and just enough heat to set your kindle on fire.

If you enjoyed this book please follow her on Amazon or Facebook for alerts when more books are released - Click here for her Amazon Author Page.

f

Printed in Poland
by Amazon Fulfillment
Poland Sp. z o.o., Wrocław
27 April 2021

53d46553-9200-4bca-8847-132b6bbdd669R01